PENGUIN BOOKS

THE DEVIL'S LARDER

'One subversive, lyrical banquet. Disquieting yet somehow affirming, this is poetic manna for the imaginary soul, and if not from heaven, then from an even more tempting, voluptuous recess' *Observer*

'Clever and original . . . fanciful, poetic . . . wholly convincing' *Independent*

'Peculiar, funny, blunt and sad all at the same time. Crace writes with a passion and a slinky quirkiness which he sustains throughout this collection of twisted tales' *List*

'A literary dish fit for the Gods [and] all discerning readers. Beautifully written, witty . . . It is a feast' *Herald*

'Deliciously written' *Arena*

'Crace constructs modern riddles, fables, fantasies, jokes, tragedies and comedies out of food' *New Statesman*

ABOUT THE AUTHOR

Jim Crace is the author of *Continent*, which won the 1986 Whitbread First Novel Award; *The Gift of Stones*; *Arcadia*; *Signals of Distress*, awarded the 1995 Royal Society of Literature's Winifred Holtby Memorial Prize; *Quarantine*, which was shortlisted for the Booker Prize and won the 1997 Whitbread Novel Award; *Being Dead*, shortlisted for the 1999 Whitbread Novel Award and winner of the prestigious US National Books Critics Circle Fiction Award for 2000; and *The Devil's Larder*. Most of these are published by Penguin. He has also received the E. M. Forster Award, the Guardian Fiction Prize and the GAP International Prize for Literature. His books have been translated into more than twenty languages.

Jim Crace lives in Birmingham with his wife and two children. For more information about Jim Crace and his writing, please visit the unofficial website at www.jim-crace.com

The Devil's Larder

JIM CRACE

PENGUIN BOOKS

PENGUIN BOOKS

Published by the Penguin Group
Penguin Books Ltd, 80 Strand, London WC2R 0RL, England
Penguin Putnam Inc., 375 Hudson Street, New York, New York 10014, USA
Penguin Books Australia Ltd, 250 Camberwell Road,
Camberwell, Victoria 3124, Australia
Penguin Books Canada Ltd, 10 Alcorn Avenue, Toronto, Ontario, Canada M4V 3B2
Penguin Books India (P) Ltd, 11 Community Centre,
Panchsheel Park, New Delhi – 110 017, India
Penguin Books (NZ) Ltd, Cnr Rosedale and Airborne Roads,
Albany, Auckland, New Zealand
Penguin Books (South Africa) (Pty) Ltd, 24 Sturdee Avenue,
Rosebank 2196, South Africa

Penguin Books Ltd, Registered Offices: 80 Strand, London WC2R 0RL, England

www.penguin.com
www.jim-crace.com

First published by Viking 2001
Published in Penguin Books 2002
3

Set in Monotype Dante
Printed in England by Clays Ltd, St Ives plc

There are no bitter fruits in Heaven.
Nor is there honey in the Devil's larder.

Visitations 7:11

If you must ride with Hunger as your horse
then trust in Nature to provide a course.
Suck marrow from discarded bones.
Dine on the sauces of the thorn and gorse.
Lick salt on stones.

Horseman, let your reins fall light,
and ride the slow digestions of the night.

MONDAZY *(translated by the author)*

I

Someone has taken off – and lost – the label on the can. There are two glassy lines of glue with just a trace of stripped paper where the label was attached. The can's batch number – RG2JD 19547 – is embossed on one of the ends. Top or bottom end? No one can tell what's up or down. The metal isn't very old.

They do not like to throw it out. It might be salmon – not cheap. Or tuna steaks. Or rings of syruped pineapple. Too good to waste. Guava halves. Lychees. Leek soup. Skinned, Italian plum tomatoes. Of course, they ought to open up the can and have a look, and eat the contents there and then. Or plan a meal around it. It must be something that they like, or used to like. It's in their larder. It had a label once. They chose it in the shop.

They shake the can up against their ears. They sniff at it. They compare it with the other cans inside the larder to find a match in size and shape. But still they cannot tell if it is beans or fruit or fish. They are like children with unopened birthday gifts. Will they be disappointed when they open up the can? Will it be what they want? Sometimes their humour is macabre: the contents are beyond description – baby flesh, sliced fingers, dog waste, worms, the venom of a hundred mambas – and that is why there is no label.

One night, when there are guests and all the wine has gone, they put the can into the candlelight amongst the debris of their meal and play the guessing game. An aphrodisiac, perhaps: 'Let's try.' A plague – should they open up and spoon it out? A tune, canned music, something never heard before that would rise from the open can, evaporate, and not be heard again. The elixir of youth. The human soup of DNA. A devil or a god?

It's tempting just to stab it with a knife. Wound it. See how it bleeds. What is the colour of the blood? What is its taste?

We all should have a can like this. Let it rust. Let the rims turn rough and brown. Lift it up and shake it if you want. Shake its sweetness or its bitterness. Agitate the juicy heaviness within. The gravy heaviness. The brine, the soup, the oil, the sauce. The heaviness. The choice is wounding it with knives, or never touching it again.

2

'This is for the angel,' grandma used to say, tearing off a strip of dough for me to take into the yard. 'Leave it somewhere he can see.' Sometimes I left the strip on the street wall. Sometimes I draped it on the washing line. Sometimes I put it on the outside windowsill and hid behind the kitchen curtain beads to spot the angel in the yard.

Grandma said I wouldn't catch him eating the dough. 'That's only greedy birds,' she explained. 'The angel comes to kiss it, that's all, otherwise my bread won't rise.' And, sure enough, I often saw the birds come down to peck at our strip of dough. And, sure enough, my grandma's bread would nearly always rise. When it didn't she would say the birds had eaten the strip of dough before the angel had had a chance to prove it with his kisses.

But I never saw an angel on the windowsill. Not even once.

The thought of angels in the yard terrified my girls and so, when we made bread – in that same house, but thirty years along the line and grandma long since gone to kiss the angels herself – I used to say, 'To make good bread I need an angel in the kitchen. Who'll be the angel today and kiss the dough?' My girls would race to kiss the dough. I'll not forget the smudge of flour on their lips. Or how, when I had taken the scarred and toppling loaves of bread out of the oven, they'd demand a strip of hot crust to dip into the honey pot or wipe around the corners of the pâté jar. This was their angel pay. This was their reward for kissing.

Now there are no angels in the kitchen. I'm the grandma and the girls are living far too far away to visit me more than once or twice a year. I'm too stiff and out of sorts to visit them myself unless I'm taken in a car, but I don't like to ask. I stay in touch with everyone by phone. I keep as busy as I can. I clean, although the house is far too large for me. I walk, when it is warm and dry, down to the port and to the shops and take a taxi back. I keep plants in the yard in pots and on the windowsills. I eat mostly out of a can or frozen meals or packet soups.

This afternoon, I thought I'd fill my time by making bread. My old wrists ache with tugging at the dough of what, I think, will have to be my final loaves. I tore a strip off for good luck, kissed it, put it on the windowsill. I warmed the oven, greased the tins, and put the dough to cook on the highest shelf. Now I'm waiting at the window, with a smudge of flour on my lips and with the smell of baking bread rising through the house, for the yard to fill and darken with the shadows and the wings.

3

No one is really sure exactly where the restaurant might be, though everyone's agreed that the walk to reach it is clandestine and punishing but hardly beautiful. There will be hills and scooping clouds and sulphur pools to menace us. A ridge of little *soufrières* will belch their heavy, eggy breath across our route. Our eyes will run. Our chests will heave. We'll sneeze and stumble, semi-blind, with nothing but the occasional blue-marked tree trunk to guide us on our way.

But still we want to risk the walk. The restaurant's reputation is enough to get us out of bed at dawn. We have to be there by midday if we want to get back safely in the light. The five of us, five men, five strangers united by a single appetite.

We take the little taxi to where the boulder track is beaten to a halt by the river, and then we wade into the water and the trees. We're wading, too, of course, into the dark side of ourselves, the hungry side that knows no boundaries. The atmosphere is sexual. We're in the brothel's waiting room. The menu's yet to be paraded. We do not speak. We simply wade and hike and climb. We are aroused.

The restaurant is like a thousand restaurants in this part of the world: a wooden lodge with an open veranda, and terraces with smoky views across the canopy towards the coast. There is a dog to greet us, and voices from a radio. An off-track motorbike is leaning against a mesh of logs. But none of the twenty tables, with their cane chairs, are as yet occupied. We are, it seems, the only visitors.

We stand and wait. We cough. We stamp on the veranda floor, but it is not until the Austrian, weary and impatient, claps his hands that anybody comes. A woman and a boy too young to be her son. She is well-dressed, with heavy jewellery. We would have liked it better if the waiter were a man.

She has bush meats, as we'd expect, she says. Some snake which she'll kebab for us, some poacher's treats like mountain cat, and dried strips of any flesh or glands we'd dare to name. She has, she says, though it's expensive, parrot meat from a species that is virtually extinct.

What else? To start, hors d'oeuvres, she has soft-bodied spiders, swag beetles, forest roaches, which taste (according to one of our number) 'like mushrooms with a hint of gorgonzola cheese'. To drink? She offers juice or cans of beer or water flavoured in some unexpected ways.

But we have come – as well she knows – not for these rare dishes but for Curry No. 3 – the menu's hottest offering, the fetish of the hill. Back in the town, if Curry

No. 2 appears on menus, then it's clearly understood that mountain chicken is on offer, that's to say it's curried *cuissardes* of frog. But we are seeking something more extreme than frog, something prehistoric, hard-core, dangerous, something disallowed where we come from. We mean, at last, to cross the barriers of taste.

So she will bring us Curry No. 3 in her good time. It isn't done to ask what she will use for meat, although the boy is eyeing us and could be bribed, with cigarettes, to talk. We simply have to take our chances. There might be lizard in the pot or some unlisted insect, in no book. We are prepared for monkey, rat or dog. Offal is a possibility, a rare and testing part we've never had before, some esoteric organ stained yellow in the turmeric. Tree shark, perhaps. Iguana eggs. Bat meat. Placenta. Brain. We are bound to contemplate, as well, the child who went astray at the weekend, the old man who has disappeared and is not missed, or the tourist who never made it back to her hotel; the sacrificed, the stillborn and the cadavers, the unaccounted for.

And we are bound to contemplate the short fulfilment we will feel and then the sated discontent that's bound to follow it, that's bound to come with us when we, well-fed, begin descending to the coast, not in a group, but strung out, five weary penitents, weighed down by our depravities, beset by sulphur clouds, and driven on by little more than stumbling gravity.

How silent the forest is, now that our senses have been dulled by food. How careless we've become as we devour the path back to the river and the road. How tired and spent. We are fair game for any passing dogs or snakes.

Those flies and wasps are free to dine on us. Those cadavers can rise up from the undergrowth and seize us by the legs if they so wish. For we're not hungry any more. We found the path up to the restaurant and it was punishing.

4

Now I will tell you what to eat outdoors when it is dark. Cold foods will never do. The key to dining without light is steam. And cold food does not steam, excepting ice. No, you must warm the night about you with the steam of soup, a dozen foods in one. You cannot tell the carrots from the beans until you have them in your mouth. You cannot, even then, distinguish what is leek from what is onion.

The bowl should not be shallow, but deep and lipped so that what steam there is must curl and gather at the centre. The steam contains the smell. And so you warm your nose on smell, and warm your mouth on flavour, and warm your hands on bowl. You should, of course, be standing and your coat should have its collar up. You do not talk. There is no time. You have to finish what you have before the steam has gone.

Once you have finished, there is a chilling residue of

steam. It cowers in the bowl. It dares not chance the darkness and the cold. And if you do not take your hands away, and if you press your face on to the rim, and if you close your eyes so tightly that your darkness is complete, the steam and smell will kiss your lips and lids and make you ready for the slow digestion of the night.

5

If those children had been mine I would have shouted out and stopped them. But they were strangers, only passing through, and I was irritated. So I stood and watched. They'd find out soon enough.

The family had pulled their car in to my field, as if the farmland had been set aside for picnickers. Their mum and dad had spread their blankets in the shade of our horse pine, with its inviting mattress of orange needles, and sent the children off, across my land, to stretch their legs.

I've seen it all before, a dozen times. What child of five or six – as these two seemed to be – would not be drawn to our fine crab? In every way but one it is a grander tree, dramatic and more showy than any of its sweeter apple cousins on the farm. That day, as he and she in all their innocence went hand in hand across the field, the fruit was at its best, in clumps as tightly packed as berry strigs, and ripening unevenly on its crimson pedicels through all the blushing harvest colours, yellow and orange to purple-red.

My crab's a vagrant, seeded more than thirty years ago, by some rogue animal no doubt, and not put there – as all the creaky grandads claim – by a bolt of lightning souring ground where lovers from opposing villages were kissing. 'That's why the fruit is bitter,' they say. And that explains the blush.

To these two youngsters, as they reached the crab, it must have seemed they'd found a magic tree, with all the warmer tints and shades of a paintbox or Christmas coloured lights or some exaggerated textile print, and with such low branches that all they had to do was help themselves.

I watched them reach up to the lowest fruit and hesitate, a warning trapped behind my teeth. At first they touched but did not pick. This surely must be theft. Such tempting treats could not be free. Besides, they were not sure what kind of fruit it was. They'd not seen these on supermarket stands or in their gardens. Too small to be an apple, too large to be a rosehip. Too hard, despite its cone-like oval shape, to be a plum tomato. The open bases of the fruit were hairy and protruding like on a pomegranate. Yet these were clearly not pomegranates. At last, they pulled the fruit down from the tree. Here was their perfect contribution to the family picnic. Their harvest would, they knew, be irresistible.

But first, of course, they each rubbed an apple against their clothes, to get a shine, and (almost at my silent prompting) tasted it. My mouth was watering. I saw the children shake their heads and spit. They'd never pass a crab again without their unforgetting mouths flooding with distaste.

I did not stay to watch their picnicking. There's always work to do. But I imagine that, when they sat cross-legged on their fine blankets beneath the pine while mum and dad dished out a harmless meal from plastic containers, tin foil and flasks, the children brought the food up to their mouths with just a touch of fear and half a glance towards the tree that had betrayed their hopes. Here was a lesson never to be forgotten, about false claims, and bitterness, and trespassing.

Sometimes, in a certain mood, I walk down to the bottom fences of my land, where my gate, ever open on to the road, gives access to picnickers, and find myself a little sad that no small child is running, full of hope, across the field. Then the small child that still survives in me shoves me in the back. I walk across to taste the fruit of that one crab for myself. I never swallow any of the flesh, of course. I simply plunge my teeth into the tempting bitterness. Even after all these years – misled, misled, misled again – I like to test the flavours of deceit. And I still find myself surprised by its malicious impact in my mouth. It's bitter-sweet and treacherous, the kiss of lovers from opposing villages.

6

It was Monday, almost noon, and he still suffered from the aftermath of Sunday's garlic. Bad breath and a stinking conscience, too.

He walked about the offices as usual, distributing client folders and the gossip, leaning over colleagues at their desks. He noticed how their heads went back, an instant recoil from his face, his speech. He noticed how their hands went up to hide their mouths and noses. He noticed how they frowned at him.

Was there some unexpected tangent from his working life that touched the private circle of his friends? He racked his brains and found no link. They could not possibly have heard how badly he'd behaved the night before, how slyly and how grossly. They could not know what harm he'd done. No, the disapproval that his colleagues were so obviously displaying had to be intuitive, instinctive, from the heart. The evidence of his misdeeds was hanging round his shoulders like a heavy, garish shroud, he guessed. He shrugged it off. Raised his voice. Would not lose face.

7

Our merchant-traders' club behind the warehouses is still
better known to members as 'the Whistling Chop'. Here's
why. Soon after it was founded in the 1870s by the great-
grandfather of our present mayor, the resident manager
came out of his office one evening to find a waiter in the
corridor carrying a tray of food. A not unusual sight.
Except that this waiter had gravy on his chin. The man
had helped himself to some of the cut chicken breast
intended for the members in the dining rooms. 'Not only
is this common theft,' the manager said, 'it's also un-
hygienic in the extreme. If the gentlemen had required
dirty fingers in their meal, they would have ordered them.
And had they wanted you to join them here for dinner,
they would have had a card delivered to your home.'

The waiter lost his job, of course. But sacking him was
not enough for the club manager. He was a man who
prided himself on his systems. And clearly these were

failing. How many waiters helped themselves to members' food, he wondered. How many meals were so diminished and defiled before they reached the tables? How could he put an end to it?

He chuckled when the answer came to him. A sharp idea. A witty one. He added his new rule to the list on the staffroom door: 'During their passage from the kitchens to the dining rooms with members' orders of food and drink, all waiters are directed to whistle. Any break in whistling longer than that required to draw breath will attract a fine or a dismissal.'

Now he could sit inside his office, the door a touch ajar, and monitor the traffic to the dining rooms. He got to recognize the waiters from their whistling. There were the warblers, who merely offered a seamless trill without a melody. And then there were the songsters, addicts of the operetta and the music hall, or country lads with harvest tunes. One waiter specialized in hymns. Another always piped the wedding march, a touch too fast. There were, as well, the irritating ones, who sounded either as if they'd lost their dogs, or as if they were impatient stationmasters.

Nevertheless, the manager adored his latest rule. It was the cleverest control he'd ever exerted over his employees. He'd stopped them eating members' meats for free and also, he judged, he'd caused the waiters to appear a little foolish to themselves. And that was no bad thing.

The members liked the system, too. It jollied up their club. And there was always early warning when their food was on its way. A risqué anecdote or some recent slander could be put on hold until the waiter had come and gone. A gentleman, dining quietly in a private room with someone other than his wife, might be glad to hear the wedding march approaching and be grateful for the chance to disengage.

All very satisfying, then, until the day the manager discovered gravy on the palm of his own hand and on his shirt cuff. Still slightly warm. It smelled – and tasted – of lamb, that day's select dish. It was a mystery. He'd not been in the kitchens for an hour or so. He'd not been in the dining rooms. He'd only been upstairs, replacing magazines and newspapers in the reading lounge. He retraced his steps, but found no clues until he was coming down again and held on to the bottom stair-post to swing himself into the service corridor, like some hero in a play, his private vanity. Again, his hand was dark with meat.

It was not clear to him at once why there should be fresh gravy on the flat top of the post. It was just possible, he supposed, that there was some innocent explanation, a spill perhaps. But, still, he would be vigilant.

For the next day or two, he took to stepping to his office door and peering down the corridor whenever he heard whistling. At last his worst fears were confirmed. A waiter passed, a tray of lunches poised above his shoulder. But still there was the pungent smell of pork hanging in the corridor. The man had left a nice chop on the stair-post. He would have eaten it during his unwhistling return had not the manager waylaid him with his dismissal papers and thus robbed the club of selections from *The Scarlet Veil*.

A tougher system was required, of course. The waiters were now called upon to whistle on their way back to the kitchens with their empty trays as well as on their journeys out. It was a step too far. The service corridor was bustling now with competing and discordant tunes. The members seemed discomforted as well. One wrote an unsigned paragraph in the complaints ledger. He said the club had begun to sound 'like a public alleyway' and not a refuge where merchants and traders might come to find a little peace. Another told the manager, 'You've turned the place into an orchestra pit.'

The manager had one last card to play. He could not ask the waiters to whistle without cease whenever they were working. They served nine-hour shifts. Nor could he sack the waiters and require the members to collect their meals themselves. That might suit the spirit of democracy, which was fashionable in the town at that time, but would not please his businessmen. Instead, he took upon himself the job of carrying dishes and servers of meat only along the corridor into the dining rooms. The members could then help themselves to as much as they wanted, as many chops, as much carved beef, as great a number of chicken wings as they could despatch at one sitting. So they were satisfied.

The waiters provided all the other services, of course. The manager could not do everything, nor could he be expected to have eyes in the back of his head. He had to trust his waiters ultimately. He was past caring if they helped themselves to vegetables on the way along the corridor, or poked their tongues into the soups. His main tasks had been to save the flesh and stop the whistling. He had succeeded, too. He was, though, once in a while and much to his alarm, tempted himself in that dim corridor by all the smells and flavours of the meat. And, at those times, a colleague on the staff might catch him whistling, as small boys do to help them cope with their remorse.

8

If Anna was allergic to aubergines she hadn't noticed. She was unhesitant in buying them and cooking them and eating them. On shop display their plumpness and their waxiness were irresistible, though, honestly, the flavour was too tart sometimes. A pinch of sugar helped. But tartness is often the price you have to pay for beauty. She'd learned that lesson from too many of her friends.

Her symptoms were discreet: a little flushing, possibly a touch of wind, and occasionally – following a dinner party or a late meal out – what her mother called a flighty head, but nothing sinister or even inconvenient. She did not suffer from rashes or palpitations. There were no seizures. So she had little opportunity to discover that aubergines did not suit her, that aubergines were treacherous and damaging. They seemed to her too flawless to be harmful, too pleasing to the eye. She liked the aubergine's affinity with olive oil and garlic, its generous response to mushrooms or tomatoes. It kept good company. She liked its versatility, just as happy to be stuffed as fried, just as tasty in a moussaka or a ratatouille as in a dip or served as fainting priest.

Anna took the usual precautions in her kitchen, of course, cutting off the bruises and the sponge, scooping out the pips and degorging the bitterness in a saltwater soak, before she put the fruit into its saucepan or its dish. She had been told that it was bad luck to slice an aubergine lengthways or peel an aubergine. Good fortune came to those who favoured cubes, or wheels of fruit, rimmed with blue-black tyres of rind. Indeed, she'd lived a life of good fortune and good health, she thought.

She was well into her seventies before her joints seized up. Then even simple tasks – like cubing aubergines – became a challenge and a cause of pain. She had a walking stick for use inside the house. 'You should give up the toxic foods,' her younger and exquisite neighbour said, 'or else you'll stiffen up completely. Your fault!'

What were 'the toxic foods'? The neighbour listed all the usual suspects – pickles, citrus fruits, bananas, fat milk and cheese, red meat, green meat, tomatoes, coffee, chocolate, shore fish, cheap wine, rhubarb – and then she raised her knife to stab the little lunchtime stew that Anna, despite her aches and pains, had prepared for both of them. 'These aubergines. They're poisonous. They'll have to go. They're why your wrists and knees have let you down.' They left their meal unfinished on their plates.

Anna made adjustments to her life. She never asked her neighbour back for lunch again. The woman was too poisonous, she thought. Despite herself, she cut down on the coffee that she drank. She ate less meat and fewer oranges. But Anna liked her aubergines too much. She was undisciplined. She meant to give them up, but when she saw them – purple, polished – in the shops, she soon forgot about her allergy and all the damage it had caused. She scooped and cubed and wheeled until she had to use her stick out in the street as well. She grew old and frail unnecessarily. Just a little self-restraint, a little less regard for comeliness, may well have kept her younger, quicker, straighter than her years.

9

Whenever a liner or the ferry put in to port, we'd end up at the Passenger Bar to gawp at all the trippers disembarking. Many of them would troop into the bar for something to calm their sea-churned stomachs and steady their legs. The Passenger was the first safe place that they'd encounter between the gangways and the town. Often, there were foreign girls whom we could tease and irritate. Sometimes there was a tourist looking for a guide, or a businessman wanting a local to translate for him, or simply someone needing two strong arms to carry luggage to the hotels. Perhaps – as happened once before, a hundred years ago – one of the older women passengers (a German probably) would pay for sex. Their fees would subsidize our studies.

So we – the five of us – would leave our work and gather in the Passenger at the funnel blast of every approaching ship. We'd take the large, square table by the door, buy beer that we could hardly afford, dine gratis on the bar's salt-glazed, thirst-inducing snacks, and wait for prey. We had a trick to play on them.

My colleague Victor and I had been working all year on the chemical properties of carbonated drinks. We hoped to isolate the tingling discharge on the tongue, the mild but disconcerting pain-with-pleasure response that follows every sip of sparkling water or fizzy fruit drink or champagne, and create a sweet food coating from which the pain had been removed. Succeed and patent it, then we'd be rich, we thought.

We understood the mechanisms, how receptors in the mouth parried the assault of dissolved CO_2 with their defensive saliva, how legions of enzymes reacted with the sparkle to produce a complex carbonic acid, our guilty irritant. And we had succeeded in blocking this effect with neutralizing dorzolamides. We'd tested what remained on rats and noted that our tincture, oddly, made them sneeze. We tasted it ourselves, the merest dab on our tongues. Instead of the familiar fizz and the ambiguous shudder of pleasure, instead of the rodent sneeze, we responded with a sudden, unearned laugh, real to the ears, but mirthless in its derivation. Every time we tested it, the outcome was the same, an involuntary reflex of laughter, independent of the will. We had concocted the inverse of an onion, bringing emotionless joy instead of tears. We called our mixture the sternly, scientific-sounding 'euphrosyne', after the Muse who 'rejoices the heart'.

I must blame Victor for the sin of breaking scientific protocol. He bought some snacks and coated them with fluid euphrosyne. These days, he'd be struck off the register for being so dangerously unprofessional. But that day, as soon as we were summoned by funnel blasts, we hurried to the Passenger for our first consumer trials. Our snacks, of course, replaced the ones provided by the bar on our table.

Two Canadian travellers with rucksacks, young men about our own age, were easily tempted to join us. We even bought them beers and were unusually attentive. The volume of their laughter after they had, almost simultaneously, stretched across to try the snacks was startling. As were their blushes and the disconcerted expressions on their faces. Perhaps we'd overdosed the euphrosyne. But, certainly, their hoots of unamused laughter briefly halted every conversation in the bar and, even after some minutes of relative silence, the Passenger's proprietor was still looking anxiously towards our group. Perhaps it was the five of us, rib-clutching and bent double at the Canadians' ersatz joviality, that made him shake his head.

It was not long before all the staff and all the regulars in the bar were privy to our secret, co-conspirators, eager for the sudden outbursts of strangers at our table. The hungry, seasick travellers, no matter how deep their oceanic melancholy, their homesickness, their dislocation, could be counted on to pop a laughter snack in their mouths to thrill us all – and both scare and animate themselves – with their shocking chemical mirth. It must have seemed we hosted the jolliest bar table in the world. Sometimes, one of the locals took our dish of snacks and offered it around the bar. Then there'd be a salvo of laughter, like an erratic firecracker. And once, when the Passenger's proprietor was absent at a funeral, we filled every dish in the bar with euphrosyne snacks and punctuated that afternoon, down at the harbourside, with the intermittent rifle blast of gladdened, triggered customers who had not thought to laugh so readily amongst so many strangers. We never tired of it.

Regrettably, I am not rich. Euphrosyne was widely tested but considered unmarketable. Consumers do not like to lose control. Besides, a food which causes sudden laughter in company is likely to be expelled on to other people's plates and jackets. No commercial company would take the risk. And that's a shame. I feel we could have made the world a more amusing place. What scientist can claim more?

I always told my children, at times of stress, that 'laughter is the best medicine', that one good joke is equal to an hour in the gym. It must have been tiring having a scientist as a father. So, usually, I bit my tongue to suppress all the tedious proofs and details at my fingertips – the eighty-seven muscles that were employed every time they laughed; the aerobic exercising of the thorax and the diaphragm; the faster heartbeat occasioned by a simple laugh; the increase of oxygen levels in the blood; and, best of all, the release of endomorphins in the brain, making anyone that cachinnates feel good about themselves.

One day, I'll dig my student papers out and, maybe, try again with euphrosyne. Not as a gloss for snacks or packaged food. But as a stimulant. I saw enough glad and startled faces in the Passenger those many years ago to know what unexpected pleasure I might bring to strangers.

10

In this part of the world, where manac beans grow as commonly and readily as moss, coddled by the salty coastal air and the nipping temperatures of night, no one with any money would choose to add them to their stews or use their greyish flour in their baking. Manacs are 'the poor man's weeds'. That is to say, they're food for pensioners, peasants, paupers and livestock. To buy a kilo in the stores is to advertise your misfortune, or to boast the recent purchase of a sow.

Yet my neighbour's daughter tells us that the well-heeled ladies who often drive past the farmers' market, where she works, on the way up to their villas in the hills have started stopping off for bags of manac beans. 'That's really slumming it,' she says. 'Next thing, they'll be having all our turnip tops. Our pigs'll have to swill on caviar.'

I think I've guessed the actual motive of these women, though. They're poisoning their husbands, in a way.

They're looking for a break in their routines. About two weeks ago, driving into town, I heard a radio report on livestock infertility and impotence. Stud animals, it said, would not perform reliably if fed on feeds which were rich in iogranulates. They'd suffer from fibrous swellings in the urinary and reproductive tracts. Even though their testes might swell to twice their normal size and the penis could enlarge appreciably, they would have problems with presenting an erection. Feeds to avoid in excess were brassicas, root grass and certain pulses.

I hardly paid attention, until I heard the radio presenter's final words. Medical records from the famines and recessions of the thirties, when manac beans became a staple foodstuff, he said, showed a tripling of impotence referrals and genital swellings amongst men from humble backgrounds. Manac beans, he warned, were 'marginally addictive' and contained the highest concentrate of iogranulates in any vegetable.

My neighbour's daughter, obviously, is overjoyed to hear my explanation for the sudden vogue for manac beans. She says it's brightened up her day. She's keen to play her part. She carries produce from her stall to the curled-down windows of the cars, looks down on to the nyloned knees, the painted nails, the bracelets and the little skirts of women from the hills, and passes over bags of toxic, regulating manacs. As evening comes and she is packing up her stall, the husbands hurry home in their long cars, their cocks enlarged, their testicles like coconuts, and with nothing to present to their ever-patient, ever-thankful wives except a firm and growing appetite for beans.

II

Here, after midnight on the seventh floor, room service is provided by a refugee. Her name – unlikely consonants, and then too many vowels – is printed on an apron tag. Her face is fiery, peppered by the many sweets she sucks from 'late till six', as she sits on her hard chair at what the waiters call the bus station. It is her job to collect the ordered trays of food and drink from the service hatch and take them down the corridors – now reeking of cigars, cheap scent and cannabis, and far from silent with the clatterings of one-night stands and thoughtless television sets and arguments – to restless, needy men who ought to be in bed asleep. A man, awake beyond midnight, is unpredictable.

The refugee – let's not attempt to say her name – is only meant to place the tray outside the room, knock lightly on the door, and disappear. Those are the rules. Wise rules. A dark hotel is ruinous. No close contact between the bus girls and the guests is tolerated. No touting for gratuities. No entry to the rooms. No extra services. They have to come and go unseen, discreet and tedious as nuns. Before the rules were imposed, a girl had been attacked, and many had been bribed or groped or compromised. One girl, on the second floor, had been a part-time prostitute. She'd tucked her business card into the napkin on each tray and done quite nicely for herself. Another one had sold thin reefers to the regulars. A third, invited into rooms for God knows what, had stolen watches, wallets, credit cards. A fourth, just for the hell of it, had helped herself to shoes and dropped them down the lift shaft for rats to eat and ghosts to wear.

Sometimes, of course, the bus girl on the seventh floor cannot avoid the guests. They have to pass her as they come and go. Or else she finds them waiting at an open door. And then she says *good morning*, and *goodnight*, *excuse me, thank you, please, goodbye* – but that is almost all she says or understands. She has, however, learnt the menu words for those occasions when the men don't use their telephones but come along the corridor and try to order food through her. *Club sandwich* comes out almost perfectly. The choices of coffees, beers and snacks are quickly recognized. *Champagne. Fish chowder. House burger and a side of fries. Rice salad with a pork brochette.* She can recite a list of fourteen whiskies. She's tasted all of them.

But ask her anything about herself and she will turn a deep and helpless red. She cannot understand, she cannot say, she cannot tell her story, what has happened to her home, her village and her family. She shakes her damaged face at these late men but nothing tumbles out. There are no words inside the pepper pot except the words for hotel food.

So, then, how can she tell the man who occupies suite 17 on Tuesday nights that she's in love with him, that she has fallen for the suppers on his service tray and is seduced by what he wants to eat? He always orders open sandwiches, sweet salad, and the sort of hinting, aromatic tea that, normally, a woman drinks.

How can she tell the gentleman how much she hates the corridors? She doesn't have the vowels or consonants.

In the closing hours of the night, when it is quiet, she has to tour the seventh floor, collecting trays and crockery and anything that's left outside the rooms. There's always bread for her to eat and untouched vegetables, sometimes a piece of meat or cheese, some fries, some long-cold soup. She puts the almost empty bottles to her mouth. She licks the liqueur glasses clean. Once in a while, if she's in luck, she's drunk by dawn on other people's dregs. And then – her shift fast coming to an end – she snoozes at the bus station and dreams, rehearsing what she'll need to say to change, to resurrect her life. Despite wise rules, the day must come when she'll have the opportunity to go through doors. All of the doors that have been shut on her. A corridor of locked and bolted doors. The door to suite 17. The door to all those hazards and gratuities.

And if she ever dares to knock and wait until the door is opened, when it swings, when all the light from outside is let in, then she will not be lost for words, not in her dreams. She will not turn a deep and helpless red. She'll see herself reflected in the bathroom's steamy mirrors, wrapped in the hotel's thick white towels, feet up before the television set. She'll see herself propped up by cushions on the bed. Beyond the perfume and the smoke, the man is waiting on her with a tray.

Her new life seems a long way off. Ten thousand trays away. Meanwhile, she mutters to herself and practises vocabulary with all the items she can name: dressed prawns, Jack Daniel's, chowder, salt, a single glass of dry white wine, champagne. *Club sandwich* comes out almost perfectly again. She orders for herself – another dream – the sort of hinting, aromatic tea that, normally, a woman drinks. She says *good morning*, to the places she has lost. And *goodnight* too. *Excuse me. Thank you. Please. Goodbye.*

12

Eggs, thank heavens, are still plentiful, though not cheap. We buy them sanctioned with the guarantee, printed on their cartons, that:

These eggs have been produced by hens that are
Protected from extremes of heat and cold;
Free from hunger and thirst;
Free to range and forage on green pasture from dawn to dusk;
Free from pain, injury and disease;
Free from fear and distress;
Free from discomfort;
Free to express themselves.

In these hard times, in these slow months between the winter and the rain, we are reduced to sharing eggs, a three-egg omelette for the six of us, fried eggs divided into two or three for sandwiches, a family meal of rice with grated cheese and a single egg for flavouring, or soft-boiled eggs, two children to each spoon. We have developed ways of making do.

We sit at night around the single gas ring in the kitchen, our plates wiped dry with bread, discussing endlessly the greater times ahead, how our misfortunes cannot last for good. We dream of work and cash and ranging free. The day will come when there is sunshine in the yard, when all our offspring will be well.

We stay at home and contemplate the life of hens.

13

It was their honeymoon – and they were bored. Bored by arguing. It had been understood, she'd thought, that he'd be patient for a month or so while she got used to all the flesh on flesh of marriage. Not intercourse. There was no intercourse as yet. They had agreed on that. But sleeping in the same bed as a man. Taking off her clothes in company. Bathing with an open door. Getting used to his endearments. He promised her that she could take her time. He said that it would be a joy for him to wait.

He was forty, and an oddity – a farmer's son who'd taught for years at the *conservatoire*. He had been married once before. His new bride, Rosa, was twenty-three. She'd been his music pupil and was – they all admitted it – too timid for her age. The flute was just the instrument for her.

They'd hired a cottage on the coast. It was September. Warm enough to swim by day. But cold at night. The village was an hour's walk away and awkward to reach by car. They realized at once that they had not brought enough provisions for the week. No matter, he said. His idea was that they could hunt for food, and eat only – well, mostly – what they had found. He had his father's sporting rifle in the car, and in the cottage there were some fishing nets, a book on fungi, and a herbal, *Mrs Caraway's Guide to Medicinal, Culinary & Cosmetic Plants*. They wouldn't use the cooker in the cottage. They'd hunt for wood and make a fire in the open grate. Firelight was romantic. And flame-cooked food was wonderful. He'd been a Scout.

It would be amusing to find the free food of the country-side, he promised Rosa, while she was letting down and brushing out her hair on their first night alone. But more than that. They would be bonded by their efforts. Her hair was lifting with the static off her brush. Her music teacher's face was in the mirror at her shoulder. He put his arms around her waist. He took her ear entirely in his mouth. He pushed himself against her back. 'It will be fun,' he said.

She was nervous in the night – the sea, the darkness and the wind – and so was glad to have his arm across her waist and resting on her chest. His penis was enlarged, but that was only natural, he said. She should ignore it. He would too. Marriage was for life and so there was no need for haste. She was delighted to be woken by the breakfast tray, though there was only tea, a slice of wedding cake, and some blackberries that he had 'hunted' in the cottage grounds.

They spent their first morning looking for fuel. There were two seams of driftwood running along the beach.

The lower seam had been dropped by the last tide. It was damp and dark and wrapped with weed. It would smoke, not burn, he said. He took her hand and led her to the upper seam of driftwood, amongst the back-beach weeds and clumps of samphire. Would she collect the wood while he went looking for some meat or fish? His hand was on her bottom, bunching up her skirt. He kissed the corner of her mouth. She felt the hard end of his tongue. Was she excited by his kiss, or terrified? Her heart was drumming on her chest.

Rosa was quite happy on the beach, alone. It was not long before she had their basket filled. The wood was dry and silvery and, somehow, was less heavy than it ought to be, as if its sinew had been hollowed out by worms. Every piece seemed worked and sculpted. The sea and sand had taken off the splinters and sharp edges. She held some to her lips and nose. It was warm and scentless. Here was a goose head with knot-hole eyes. Here was a lizard with five legs. Here was a boomerang.

That night, they dined on bread and samphire and the pigeons that he'd shot. He plucked and gutted them while she attended to the fire. The driftwood burned a salty green and blue at first but soon the light was golden from the flames. They wrapped the birds in foil and cooked them on an oven tray in the embers of the driftwood. They boiled the samphire in a camping pot. And then, cross-legged, their plates held in their laps, and cuts of bread draped over their knees like peasant serviettes, they ate their first meal alone as a married couple. Their entertainment was the food, and then the flames. The evening was not spoiled when he lay down and put his head – and nose – into her lap, the doting spaniel, and whispered to the folds and pleats of her skirt. Nor was it spoiled – in bed and in the middle of the night – when he pushed up her nightdress, pulled down his own pyjamas and wrapped himself around her like a cashew nut. She should ignore him, he had said. And that is what she did. He hardly cost her any sleep.

Next day, he left her with the basket on the dunes, while he went off with nets. He did not kiss her on the lips before he walked away. His mood had changed.

That evening, they sat a foot apart in front of the fire and dined on mackerel, grilled in mustard sauce. The enamelled fish skins pulled off like paper. The flesh was oily white. She'd never tasted fish as good. Then there were stewed blackberries and crab apples for dessert, with tinned cream, and the last slice of their wedding cake. They did not speak. Again their entertainment was the flames.

He was the first in bed that night and he pretended to be sleeping when Rosa came upstairs into the attic room. But he was watching her, she knew. Only one eye was shut. He watched her at the mirror combing out her hair. He watched her rubbing aloe cream into her face and throat. She went to urinate and clean her teeth and every sound she made was shared by him. He hardly breathed when she switched out the lamp, took off her clothes by moonlight, and hung them, with her underwear on top, across the wooden footboard of the bed. The bedroom smelled of mackerel, she thought. He'd turned his back to her. He was a cashew wrapped around himself. She said goodnight. She patted him on his shoulder. She did not know how long he lay awake because the sea air had made her tired and she was soon asleep. She did not wake to breakfast on a tray. This was day three. 'You'd try the patience of a saint,' he said when she was still in bed at ten o'clock. She found this judgement pleasing in some way.

He did not leave her on the beach alone. His bad temper needed company, and witnesses. Instead, he helped her with the wood and – as he'd done when he was teaching flute – took too many opportunities to touch her arm, her waist, her hair. He was much noisier than her. He stamped on the larger pieces until they splintered. He kicked the broken driftwood into piles, then threw it up the beach into the open basket.

'Come on,' he said. They had agreed to take the kitchen bucket and some nets a little way along the coast where there were pools – and shrimps, they hoped. Rosa followed him, carrying her shoes and stepping in his puddled footsteps. The sun came out when they were halfway down the beach. Her shadow jogged ahead of her and clipped her husband's heels. He took his shirt off and hung it over his shoulder.

They did not have much luck with shrimps. The tide was going out. He pulled his trousers up above his knees. She tucked her skirt into her knickers and waded into the sea. They needed to go deeper for the shrimps, her husband said. He went back to the beach and took his trousers off and then his underpants. She watched him from the shallows as he ran into the water. She had not seen him quite so naked before. He did not stop until he was waist deep, amongst the furthest rocks, and then he concentrated on the shrimping.

'There's hundreds here,' he said. 'Come over, Rosa. Bring the bucket.'

'It's deep,' she said.

'Take off your clothes like me. Come on, I need the bucket now. I've got our dinner here.'

She didn't take her clothes off, though. She waded in fully clothed. Her skirt worked loose and spread out around her like a picnic rug. She hid behind the bucket while he shook the shrimps out of the net.

He let her peel and wash the shrimps. They ate them at the table with bread and mayonnaise. They didn't bother with a fire that night. And he did not bother to join her in the bed. 'It's all impossible,' he'd said.

It was raining in the morning. Rosa kissed his forehead when she found him curled up on the kitchen chair. She made him breakfast. She made it clear that they should start their honeymoon again. They walked into the woods, their arms around each other's waists. He took the gun. She carried the herbal and the book on fungi in a plastic bag. He shot a pheasant, though he could have caught it with his hands. 'Poaching is not theft,' he said. Rosa filled her plastic bag with hazelnuts and blackberries (again). She checked the herbal for which plants were edible. There were some brown-cap mushrooms growing in a stand of birch trees. And there were dragon pulses growing in abundance in the lane, and rock lavender for stuffing the pheasant. The seashore wormwood was not edible. The autumn squill was far too small. The seablite was described by *Mrs Caraway* as poisonous.

There was what Rosa took to be a kind of thistle growing in the dunes. She broke a piece off. Its stem was glaucous.

41

Its leaves were leathery. She searched for it in *Mrs Caraway* but it was him – his chin upon her shoulder – who spotted the tiny illustration. Not thistle then. But sea holly or *eringo*.

'You can eat the roots,' she said.

He took the book and read the entry. 'It's good for flatulence. It's diaphoretic, aromatic and it's expectorant.' And then, 'An aphrodisiac. "The roots should be first candied or infused with fruits and then consumed. It will be witnessed how quickly Venus is provoked."'

They pulled a few handfuls of the root. They couldn't tell from smelling it how it would taste. At least they wouldn't suffer from flatulence, he said, and flatulence was always a risk with unhung pheasant.

He grated the eringo and boiled it with a little water; then he added blackberries and sugar. 'Let's see,' he said. He dipped his little finger in the bowl. He could hardly taste the root. It was too bland for him. Besides, he hadn't made it for himself. He gave the bowl to Rosa.

She used a spoon. 'It isn't very nice,' she said. 'A bit too sharp.' She was sweet-toothed.

He added some more sugar and offered her another spoonful, like a parent doling out medicine.

'It doesn't taste of anything,' she said. No thanks, she didn't want it as a sauce to eat with the roasted pheasant and the mushrooms.

He said it would be pleasant to sit naked by the fire. He coaxed her to remove her clothes. The semi-darkness and the lisping firelight made it easier for her to do as she was asked. He wrapped his arm around her shoulders. 'I know you'll need to take your time,' he said. 'I do not want to hurry you. But it *is* only natural that I should want to love you fully, on our honeymoon.' Her back was cold. Her knees and breasts were burning hot. The cushions were not comfortable. She was relieved when he suggested that they went to bed. She let him cup her breasts in his hands, although his fingers smelt of pheasant feathers. She let him curl around her with her nightdress bunched up underneath her arms. He was exasperated – and murderous – when, almost at once, she fell asleep.

It was midnight when Rosa woke. She'd dreamed that she was drowning. And, indeed, her pillow and her hair were soaking wet, and hot. Her body too. Her mouth seemed gummed with phlegm. She had to swallow. Her breasts were hard. She knew that it was something that she'd eaten. The mushrooms, perhaps. Or the pheasant had been off. But she could taste the blackberries. It was eringo that had woken her. She pushed the bedclothes on to her husband's side and lay on the bed with nothing but her nightdress for warmth. Her breathing was becoming thin and papery. She thought that she would either tear or be dissolved.

And then, quite suddenly, her fever cleared. The air expanded round her. There was space. She swung one leg over the side of the bed. She pushed the other deep into the blankets. Her body was the temperature of blood. Her breathing thickened. Her back arched. She seemed to swell and lift. She had to press her hands on to her abdomen to keep herself from floating. She had to brace her arms and thighs to stop herself from sinking through the bed. She felt like the driftwood she had gathered on the beach – compact and dry and silvery and, somehow, not as heavy as she ought to be, as if her insides had been tunnelled out by worms. And one by one – with her fingers pressed into her flesh, and with her knees spread out to make a rhombus of her legs – her splinters and her corners were removed and she became a lizard with five limbs, and she became a boomerang, and she became a root.

Rosa was up before her husband woke. She could not bear to interrupt his sleep or look at him. She wanted privacy. She made herself some tea and took it, with a spoon and the half-empty bowl of grated eringo, blackberries and sugar, into the living room. There was a little warmth left in the fire. She wrapped a tablecloth around her shoulders, and pulled a stool up to the ashes. She finished off the eringo. She licked the bowl. During the night the root had marinated with the berries. She could detect a taste like chestnuts and the pungency of quicklime.

In the early afternoon, she walked down to the beach for firewood. Her husband had gone off to get some eggs and milk from the farm. He said the free food of the countryside had been a disappointment. They'd been naive. He could not wait to have her back home where things between him and his bride could settle down, could grow. This time she recognized the symptoms when they came. Her hair and skin were soaking wet, exactly as before. Her mouth was full of spit, and then was dry and papery. She lay down on the dunes and waited, while her breathing thinned and thickened.

Rosa pulled some roots again that day, for supper. She woke at two o'clock – a little later than the night before, but no less memorably. She took an early breakfast by the fire.

She pulled more roots to take back from their honeymoon, and hid them in the car. She'd try what *Mrs Caraway* had recommended and candy them in baked syrup. She'd have to share them with her husband, she supposed. She'd have to share with him what she had found out on her own. But not just yet. Marriage was for life, she reminded herself. There was no need for haste. It would be a joy to make him wait. She'd not be caught as easily as pigeons, pheasants, shrimps.

14

When he'd been serving in the restaurant, his party trick
had been to sing out the names of all the ninety types of
pastas, in alphabetical order, in less than three minutes,
from angel hair to ziti. It was a comic aria of food – and
usually it had earned him a round of applause from the
customers, and calls for an encore. He'd got huge tips.

Now that he was working for a bank, there wasn't much
demand for pasta, but still he liked to practise his party
trick, if only for his own amusement. Skills atrophy unless
they're cared for.

Each morning, once he'd walked to the tram stop on
the way to work, he muttered all the pastas to himself.
Usually, if he cut his timing fine, he would only have
reached cannelloni, cappelletti, cavatelli, conchiglie before
his tram arrived, a modest daily pleasure he was eager to
repeat.

15

My mother's birthday – and I'll bake a pie for her. Blind pie. The sort she baked for us when we were small, on our birthdays. The trick's revealed. I have her recipe. She wrote it down more than forty years ago, in pencil and in capitals, on the last page of her 1961 House Diary. I found it on the kitchen shelf when we were clearing her apartment, the week she died.

This much I always knew. We were allowed to watch her line the deep dish with pastry and prepare a decorated lid. We'd help her roll and paste into place the walls of dough, which divided the pie into six triangular compartments. The birthday child could choose the filling, but only 'something sensible'. Sliced fruit and dates. Leek and cheese. Chicken and onion. Pigeon and damsons. The pie was fit for almost anything. But she would never let us stay to watch the filling of the spaces. We had to giggle on the far side of the kitchen door while – now we know –

she packed five of the compartments with the chosen food and blinded the sixth segment of the pie with flour and dried beans. Then she hid the contents under the lid.

We were allowed to see her slide the pie into the middle of the oven, and wait in the kitchen for the forty minutes that it took to bake. But then, again, we had to leave and guess at what she did behind our backs, what tricks she used to make the pie so generous. But here it's written down in pencil and in capitals. The lifting of the pastry lid with its exasperated shush of steam. The careful, hot removal of the aggregate, the pebbles and clay of hardened flour and bullet beans. The filling of the blind sixth, with either the necklace or the marbles that my mother had kept hidden in her linen drawer, the ornament she'd ordered through the post, the shell purse from the seaside, the metal animal, the set of dice. And finally the dinner gong, the family gathered at the oblong table, the serving spoon, the violated pastry lid, with – almost – everybody praying for no fruit, no meat, but hoping that something costly and inedible would end up on their plates.

Not me. I used to fear my mother's pies. I hated my birthdays, too. Still do. While we were exiled from the kitchen, my sisters would torment me, twisting arms and pulling hair, just to turn my birthday sour. 'You should have been a girl,' they'd say. 'Mother only wanted girls. She said you were a curse, when you were born. She told us she could never love a boy like you. You'll see. You'll see how much she loves you when she serves the pie. You're in for a surprise.'

So I'd learned to fear the contents of the sixth, that dark and blind compartment with no edible filling. Inside there'd be, my sisters would say, a little snake for my birthday, hissing hate and steam. There'd be a smooth, black bat – well-baked – to break out of the pastry lid and hunt for warrens in my hair. There'd be a nest of cockroaches to mark my anniversary. Or a cake of melted soap, with body hairs, girls' body hairs. Or else a dry and steaming toad to sing 'Congratulations' with its dry and steaming voice. Alone, alone amongst the birthday cele-brants, I always prayed my piece of pie would not be a surprise. I know, of course, what it was I always feared the most – not gifts, not bats, not toads, but that my mother's love would prove as hard and hissing as my sisters said.

And so, too late, I plan to bake a pie for her and for my sisters on our mother's anniversary, to show I know they meant me harm. I have her pencilled recipe for guidance. I have my grievances to mix in with the pastry. I'll fill the six compartments, lid the pie, and cook it well, as well as any woman could.

I'll serve the pie myself. My hand, I know, will shake as I plunge the spoon into the pastry. I know my sisters will expect surprises, gifts. They will be surprised. There'll be no empty compartment for the birthday dead, no ornament, no snake, no necklace, and no soap. And noth-ing edible. No steam. They don't deserve sliced fruit and dates, or leek and cheese, or chicken and onion. Pigeon and damsons are too good for them. The six compartments will be full of flour and dry beans. Blind pie. The sort my mother baked when I was small.

16

More than forty years ago, in simpler times, our produce wholesaler, by way of an experiment in exotica, bought a consignment of kumquats, cheaply, off a storm-docked cargo boat. Well, cheaply if he could pass them all on to his retailers, and quickly. Then he'd make a profit. He gave the problem of disposing of this unfamiliar fruit to his raw and unpersuasive son. But after two days of softening and maturing at the depot, the kumquats were – mostly – still unsold.

'People don't want kumquats, whatever they might be,' his son explained. 'They just want simple oranges. This isn't Paris. Don't blame me.'

'Well, give them simple oranges.'

His father took a fat black marker from his desk, and underneath the word 'KUMQUATS' on the display card, wrote 'a.k.a. PYGMY ORANGES'.

They'd made their profit by the end of the day. Pygmy

oranges were all the rage, just right for kids and snacks and picnics. They could be eaten whole. No peel, no mess, no lacquered chins. How had our town got by without this infant fruit for so long? The retailers demanded more. But our wholesaler could not discover any fresh supplies. He couldn't count on any more storm-docked boats.

'That's life,' his son said. 'Ten days ago, they didn't want to know. Today they want kumquats and won't settle for anything else. Oranges are far too vulgar now.'

'Well, give them kumquats,' his father said. 'The wholesaler should always come up with the goods.'

He took the same fat pen from his desk, found the display card for 'ORANGES', and wrote below 'a.k.a. KINGQUATS'.

He gave his son a knowing, weary look. He hoped this twice-explained lesson had been learned, that if customers were soft enough to like their oranges reduced, then they'd be bound to love their kumquats swollen and resized. This was his understanding, from a life in trade. The buying public were as innocent as kids. They'd always pay to see the scale of life disrupted by the pygmies and the kings.

17

Here is a question for your guests, next time you dine with new acquaintances at home. The coffee has been served. You sit, not quite at ease, confronted by the detritus of empty plates and by the awkwardness of strangers. You say, to break the ice, 'Imagine it. You're on a raft, the two of you, three days from any land. Everybody else has drowned. The sea is calm; it's hardly bothering the raft. The four horizons offer you no hope of rescue. The skies are absolutely blue. Bad news. Blue skies provide no rain. The empty can you've found aboard the raft will not fill up with rain before eternity. You're bound to die of thirst within three days, before there's any chance of being washed up on a shore, unless you drink. You have to make a choice. What do you drink to save your lives? Sea water, or your own urine? Will you take piss or brine? Decide. You're caught between the devil and the salt blue sea. Don't hesitate to say.'

I promise you, the woman always takes the devil. It does not bother her that piss contains her body waste, the excess, sterile toxins of her complicated life. She is at ease with body fluids, blemishes, has to be, she deals with them throughout her years. She finds salvation in herself, collects the urine in the can, and drinks.

The husband – again I promise you – selects the sea, invariably. He knows the dangers of the salt. They say it dries your blood and drives you mad. The water makes you thirstier, so you drink even more. But still a man can't face the poisons in his life. He'd rather die. He finds salvation in the seven tenths. He dips the can into the sea and drinks.

Which of the two survives, do you suppose? The woman, obviously. She must outlive the man. Her own bladder is soon empty, but the ocean is endless. Her husband's lips are white with salt, not thirst. She has a second chance through him. She makes her husband get his penis out and – despite his protests of disgust – fill the can for her. His water is quite clear. Not salty either. His kidneys have removed the salt. So long as he drinks sea, preferring universe to self, she will survive unscathed.

There are no shores. There are no rescue boats. No rain.

18

Nobody thought it wise or necessary to invite the director to my backward-running dinner party for colleagues on my twenty-seventh birthday. He was not the sort to much enjoy our kind of levity. He wouldn't be amused, we thought, by the reversals that I'd planned. I was not keen that he should see me – his ambitious protégé – in this minor, playful mood, in which digestifs came before aperitifs and cutlery was dirtied in topsy-turvy order.

But he came nevertheless, and was announced with some embarrassment by the steward at the private club room just as we were finishing cigars and Calvados and looking forward – backward? – to our meal. He indicated that we should not rise from our places; the evening was informal, and he was hungry only for some company. He had, he said, good news. For one of us.

He pulled a chair up to the angle of a table end and passed some pleasantry about it being just as well that he had missed dessert. The director took the uneasy volume of laughter which greeted his remark to be a friendly acknowledgement of his spreading waistline. We assured him – bravely frivolous – that he had not missed dessert at all. I dared not catch his eye.

The director hung his jacket over the back of the chair, accepted a small cigar and a liqueur for himself, and started to address the other seven at the table. 'I have been honoured,' he said, 'not only, of course, by your hospitality this evening but also by the Board of Governors . . .' He produced a fax from his jacket pocket and waved it at us. 'Brussels, gentlemen,' he said. 'I am to be Director Europe, Forward Planning.' We rewarded him with some applause.

'It is possible, of course, that my preferment might provide some opportunities for my young friends,' he continued. 'Which one of you gentlemen has the finest creases and the straightest back? At least one of you – I should not tease – has so impressed me with his gravitas that I can imagine him established as my aide in Belgium. And there are further possibilities. So best behaviour, gentlemen! We'll see who benefits on Monday.' He turned to place his empty glass on a side table and raised both eyebrows. 'Who knows?' he said, smiling directly at me, and 'We shall see.'

His good news silenced us. No one spoke until the trolley with desserts was brought into the room. 'Desserts?' Director Europe said. 'They're rather late.'

He put his spoon into his cream gateau. He nodded, smiled and added, 'Now I smell the flavour of the meal.' Then, 'I am reminded of my grandmother, when she was in the nursing home. I went with my older brother one evening to visit her. She'd ordered hot mint water as an aperitif and then, when the nurse had settled the tray of food across her bed, she insisted on eating her meal in reverse order, starting with chocolate mousse and ending with the soup. "I am eighty-three years old," she told me and my brother. "Life is uncertain. Eat the pudding first."'

He put the dessert spoon into his mouth and hummed with pleasure at the taste. My prospects were restored by him. Forward Planning seemed a possibility again. Outside, the waiters lined up with the meats. And, in the kitchen, our soup was simmering on low and patient flames.

I'm twenty-seven years of age today. Life is uncertain. Leave the soup till last.

19

After she had caught food poisoning from the soft cheese at the cafeteria (but before any of the symptoms had appeared), she had made love to her boyfriend and then to an old acquaintance she'd encountered entirely by chance, and then had kissed (though only playfully, but using tongues) her special friend in her local bar, a homosexual man, in fact.

She fell ill that evening, fever, headache, vomiting. And the three men caught up with her early next day. Fevers, headaches, vomiting, throughout the town.

Now, she wondered, could it be that in a world where there were evidently at least three cases of sexually transmitted indigestion, that there could be – that she could even cause – a single case of gastronomically transmitted venereal disease? Could that old devil, lurking in the bedroom, flourish in the kitchen too? Might she discover recipes to feed and satisfy and aggravate those famished lovers at her door?

20

For the 500th anniversary of the ending of the siege, Professor Myles McCormick, the big, bizarre Chicagoan who'd made our town his 'project', arranged a study week for amateur historians, ending with a celebratory feast. The fourteen participants – mostly, like the professor himself, Americans – could tour the burial site, the recently discovered (and augmented) earthworks and emplacements of the besieging army, the museum with its sad collection of wills and testaments, the still-intact harbour chain that had once stretched across the sea channel to the port. They could inspect the little statue of the city prefect chewing on a shoe and the memorial obelisk with its roster of the wealthy dead. In seminars, they could consider the day-to-day minutiae of living – and dying – without fresh food for more than fifteen months, and then discuss the broader, nagging questions of historical principle. And they could read and buy (in the professor's own translation from the sixteenth-century text) the merchant dell'Ova's contemporary accounts.

The study group was surprisingly easygoing for such a mordant subject, cheerful, attentive and intelligent, delighted with the hotel and the town, and keen to be as stimulated as possible on this short, testing and expensive vacation. So Professor McCormick must have judged that they would appreciate the 'fitting' menu he'd prepared for the closing feast. The hotel chef, a Dane with an unexpected sense of humour, had volunteered his services. 'Anything for a change,' he had said. The professor presented him with a copy of dell'Ova's diaries, in which he'd highlighted one of the final passages. 'Do what you can with that.'

We have been reduced to eating slop that might have been intended for my good host's chickens and his pigs, had not those chickens and those pigs been speedily dispatched some weeks ago [dell'Ova wrote, eleven days before he died from the insupportable pain of 'hunger headaches']. I have always hoped, despite my many travels, that I would not need to sacrifice my dignity so much that I could sup on baser foods, as savages, but in these last few weeks I have discovered myself tasting – and, indeed, relishing – lascivious flesh from mice, ebb meat and worms, and also from dead creatures that have perished from their want of sustenance, all flavoured by our only condiment, the salt from shore weed. My vegetable dishes have presented only the very best grasses from the city lanes and leaves of such variety that autumn seems to have bared its branches at us in the courtyard, though it be only early spring . . . Today we were called to table and an unexpected stew of leather goods. Within the steaming tureen our spoons located the tooled remains of a once-fine saddle, cut strips of bags and purses, a bandolier with the buckles thankfully removed, and a good pair of tanned shoes, which all too late I recognized to be my own. I can report that, given my condition and the rarity of any meal, this was the finest and sweetest-smelling preparation, as good as any beef, which it has ever been my fortune to savour or to chew. Hardship and hunger sophisticate the palate and the nose.

The chef was not required to go down to the market hall. He already had provisions in the lost-property cupboard behind reception. There he selected a child's school satchel, a calfskin handbag (a little spoiled by talc and leaking biros), a half-dozen leather belts and a well-worn pair of hiking boots, already greased with dubbin and softened for the pot by a thousand walks. These forgotten trophies of hotel guests, the chef was sure, would not taste good, no matter how the leather was tricked and dramatized with stock and sauces. But, surely, an experienced cook and innovator such as himself could produce from these ingredients something passable. This leather was only tough meat, after all. It could not taste worse than the 'squirrel steak Tabasco' he'd prepared for the *fête de la chasse* some months before. Here was a challenge.

Chef's sharpest knife was not up to the task. Once he'd unpicked any stitching from the bags and belts and had removed the sole and innards of the boots, he had to use a pair of industrial scissors to render the leather into strips about a centimetre wide. These he softened for four or five hours in tepid water.

So far, this was easier than squirrel. No skinning, no boning, and nothing to eviscerate or draw. But at least the squirrel had some flavour, even though the flavour, as it turned out, was of the acorns that it had eaten and, oddly, of gunpowder. It would be easy, obviously, to spice up and vivify the leather from the many bottles on the kitchen shelves. Some jerky sauce, perhaps, some cayenne, or packet stock. But this was cheating, chef decided. And hardly 'fitting' for the celebration of a siege that had ended 500 years ago and killed three quarters of the town.

Chef turned to dell'Ova once again for inspiration, and the professor's highlighted passage. 'The salt from shore weed' would have to be his condiment. The hotel backed on to a stony beach where there was kelp and wrack in abundance.

He had of course to compromise by preparing an 'unfitting' base for the meat. It must seem edible, at least. He assembled a casserole of equal parts water and milk, with onion, turnips, carrots, chopped fennel and haricot beans, added the strips of leather and its mulch of seaweed, and left it all on a low heat, with the lid on the pan, to reduce and tenderize.

'Shoe stew', they called it in the kitchen. But on the menu card, that evening, it was described as 'ragout dell'Ova'.

Professor McCormick was generous with wine, and so his study group was game, if a little hesitant, at least to try the celebration stew. Their evening was memorable. The amateur historians held up their forks, heavy with thick leather laces, for the benefit of the professor's video camera, plus the television news crew, and the photographers from two provincial papers, who had, thanks to the hotel's PR manager, been summoned to the feast. A splendid photograph of Thomas Luken from Columbus, Ohio, and his wife Martha was reproduced in magazines throughout the world, including *Time* and, all too obviously, the *National Enquirer*. Mr and Mrs Luken were shown tugging with their teeth on opposing ends of a strip of handbag.

Did anybody really eat the stew? Some people tried, of course. The leather itself was tasteless and beyond chewing, but the gravy was delicious, as you'd expect from such a five-star chef. When the meal was over, though, and what remained had been carried to the kitchens, it might have appeared that 'ragout dell'Ova' must have had its admirers. Not one of the plates was untouched. Some, indeed, were clean. Professor Myles McCormick would write, in his report, that 'dell'Ova's conviction that men and women can develop a taste for almost anything, if the circumstances so prescribe, was more than fully proven on this occasion.'

Indeed, most of the leather had disappeared somewhere. The amateur historians had carried off their rich experience, but not inside their stomachs. They'd simply licked the gravy off and slipped their leather memories of that fine week into their pockets, or wrapped them in their napkins, or tucked them into their handbags. This was a siege they'd not forget. This was a history lesson that had made its mark. They'd had such unexpected fun.

21

A youngish man, a trifle overweight, too anxious for his age, completed his circuit of the supermarket shelves and cabinets and stood in line, ashamed as usual.

He arranged his purchases on the checkout belt and waited, with his eyes fixed on the street beyond the shop window, while the woman at the till scanned all the barcodes on his medicines, his vitamins, his air freshener, his toilet tissue, his frozen Meals for One, his tins, his magazines, his beer and his deodorant, his bread, bananas, milk, his fat-free yoghurt, his jar of decaf and his treats – today, some roasted chicken legs, some grapes, a block of chocolate and two croissants. He rubbed his thumb along the numbers embossed on his credit card, while each item triggered a trill of recognition from the till.

The till's computer recognized the young man's 'Distinctive Shopping Fingerprint' as well, the usual ratio of fat to starch, the familiar selection of canned food, the recent and increasing range of health supplements, the unique combination of monthly magazines. The pattern of the shopping identified the customer. Even before the woman at the till had swiped the credit card, the computer had lined up the young man's details – his list of purchases for the previous seven months, his credit rating, his 'Customer Loyalty Score'. It knew broadly who he was and how he lived. It could deduce what his modest rooms above the travel shop were like, how stale they were, how flowerless, how functional, how crying out for change. Here was the man whose cat had died or run away three months ago. No cat food purchased since that time. Here was the customer who had not left the neighbourhood for more than seven days in living, byte-sized memory. Last spring, he'd tried – and failed – to cut down on patisseries and sugar. Today, for once, he had resisted his usual impulse purchase of a packet of cheroots.

Computer screened a message on the woman's till: Cheroots . . . Cheroots . . . it said. Remind the customer he has not purchased cereals or cheese or vegetables this month. Remind him of our *special offers*: 12 cans of lager for the price of 10. Buy one bottle of our Boulevard Liqueur and get a second free. Remind him that time is passing more quickly than he thinks – his washing powder should be used by now, as should the contraceptives that he bought two years ago. He must need basics, such as rice and pasta, soap, toothpaste, flour, oil and condiments. Inform him of our retail schemes and that we open now on Sunday afternoons. Advise him that he ought to do more cooking for himself. He ought to tidy up and clean the bathroom tiles with our new lemon whitener. He ought to start afresh. Suggest to him he tours our shelves again. At once. For what we choose is what we are. He should not miss this second opportunity to recreate himself with food.

22

Like all the best ideas, the old man's was a simple one. Foods nourished by the heat of sunshine should be able to relinquish that same heat and that much sunshine at a later date. It is, after all, a basic law of physics that no energy is ever lost.

Wine masters always say that the better reds release their ripening summer heat as soon as they are poured. Subtle palates can detect the year by quantifying sunshine in the grape. If that's allowed, then an orange, say, matured and coloured by the sun in some hot place, must radiate as much. It should be the perfect hand warmer in winter. A southern plum, likewise, should have the knack of stewing itself in cold water. A kilo of bananas dropped into the garden pond should, for a week or two, keep the water nicely free of ice and save the goldfish from the chill. Ice cream, surely, could be softened slightly by the presence of some dates.

'There ought to be a range of packaged fruits and vegetables – Sunbeam Meals, perhaps – that cook themselves,' our old man said. 'Picnics would be transformed by such convenience. Think of the benefits for miners, trawlermen and Eskimos. I'd be a millionaire.'

The only problem he encountered was discovering the trigger to reactivate and then release the buried heat without using means that would themselves consume an equal energy. He dedicated all his time to problems such as this when he retired. We learned to live with it and him, and only thought it strange when he was glimpsed about the town on winter nights, an orange gripped in each of his blue hands.

23

Our neighbour's husband rented a strip of land and an angling hut by the river. He had no children or dog, but he had six fruit trees, some currant bushes and a plot of meadow, where he grew vegetables. I used to pass him on the way to school. In that uncertain light, he seemed the loneliest of working men, sometimes tackling the grey-brown soil with his trenching spade, sometimes sitting on the angling bench with a hand line or a short rod, sometimes struggling up the river bank with his two buckets to irrigate his vegetables, never idle, never anything but occupied, and frightening.

He'd still be on his land when I came home from school, limping on his gammy leg, and always wearing sky-blue jeans so that, even in the grimmer half-light of the afternoon, he could not disappear. I never saw him walking to or from his home. My sisters said he slept in the angling hut, washed in the river, lived on what he grew, wee'd on his lettuces, crapped on his greens, and poisoned strangers with his crops. His wife, for reasons more weighty than her loathing of his muddy boots, had not allowed him in the house for months.

Sometimes, when he caught my eye, I'd have to wave in reply, I'd have to smile – embarrassed, I suppose – despite what my parents said about avoiding him and not accepting any fruit or vegetables. Embarrassment is worse than pain, for boys.

One afternoon when I'd had to wave at him in that last year before I went away, he pulled an apple off his tree and threw it at me, high, uphill, across the meadow fence. I caught it with one hand, the crispest catch, the smack of flesh on flesh, of skin on peel. Another time, when he was working near the road, he dropped some berries into my palm. At other times, it was a handful of his manac beans or ripe shrubnuts. And then, occasionally, he'd give me something to take home 'for the table', some radishes perhaps, or a lettuce head, or – once – a fine, fat perch he'd caught.

I never tasted anything, of course. I smiled, I waved, I shouted thanks. I took his berries and his beans, his vegetables, his fish, and dropped them from the railway bridge on to the line, a half-minute from our house, then wiped away the poison and the smell of them on snatches of wet grass. At home, I'd dream of him, bad dreams. A train was hurtling down the railway line. The blood and sap of lettuce, carrots, fish and fruit were splashed across its windscreen and its wheels.

Once, though, he caught me off guard. He must have known I'd rather die than not do what he asked. He pulled a baby carrot from the row, snapped off its plume, wiped (half) the earth off on his sky-blue trouser leg, and made me eat it there and then, while he was watching from the far side of the fence. 'You have to eat it from the earth, at once,' he said. 'Or else the flavour flies away. Go on. This is the best.' And he was right. I put his dirty carrot in my mouth. I chewed, expecting bitterness. But nothing could be more delicate and sweet than that frail root. It is a taste that's stayed with me for thirty years. A carrot from the shop could not compete. It had to be the earth, I thought, that tasted good.

And so I took to finding new ways to and from the school, and I was thankful when, at the end of the year, I moved to the boarding college and never had to pass the meadow except in father's car. I don't believe I saw our neighbour's husband for a year or two, and by then he had forgotten me – so I was not obliged to wave or smile again or throw his produce on to the railway line.

I grow carrots of my own these days. I draw them from the soil before they're quite mature and eat them there and then, just like I once did at my neighbour's husband's fence, fresh-pulled and half-disguised by earth. But there's no special taste to mine. They seem shop bought and ordinary, according to my son. So now I wonder what his secret was. If it was not the flavour of the soil that made the difference, then perhaps it was the taste of fear and shame. I can't deny that he had frightened me or that I'd cheated him. Even in the grimmer half-light of the afternoon, I cannot make our neighbour's husband disappear.

But my son is young enough for simple explanations.

I've told him how the man was calling from the far side of the fence, the stooping back, the snapping plume of leaves, and how the earth was (half) removed. It could have been his gammy trouser leg that made the carrots delicate and sweet, my son suggests (for loneliness is bound to have its taste). That one swift wipe across the sky-blue cloth, he says, had left its dressing on the root.

24

Her daughters wouldn't eat. She tried to bribe them with their favourite foods. They said they had no favourite foods. She threatened them with early bed, pocket money fines, extra duties round the house, less television. That didn't work. She feared her daughters more than they feared her. So, finally, she sought advice by contacting a childcare magazine. Its doctor wrote: 'Do not forget that mealtimes should be fun. Once your daughters begin to enjoy the occasion, they will also start to love the food. Do not impose unnecessary rules, which blunt their pleasure. Try to make the food entertaining to look at and amusing to eat.'

So mother sat her children down in easy chairs in front of the television and brought their dinners in on trays. She left them to enjoy themselves. They let their food go cold. She let them take their lunches out to the playhouse in the wood and eat with their fingers, like runaways. They threw their meals into the bushes. She tried giving them only desserts to eat. They just picked at them, even though she'd marked a smiley face on the custard skin of one fruit tart with chocolate pips. She prepared pasta dishes from five different shapes and many colours, but her daughters only tried the colours and the shapes they liked and wouldn't even taste the rest.

Finally, furious with herself, exasperated by her girls, she made a pizza and scored an angry face into the cheese topping with the handle of a knife. And just to show her, the daughters ate it, every crumb. Eating mother's anger was good fun.

25

I'll come to lunch, but only if you promise me that there'll be other guests, old friend. We've spent too many years at that oak table in your yard with just ourselves for company. And I've grown bored. Enough, I say. Let's change our habits or let's call a halt. We die too soon.

I see you wince. But, no, I'm bored by me, not you. You always were the perfect host, a listener. And I have been the less-than-silent guest for far too long. I've heard my anecdotes too many times. I can't resist repeating jokes and telling you again my views on art or gardening or God or politics or chemistry or how you comb your hair. I have a reputation, I'm mortified to say, for being the life and soul of any gathering. I'll speak my mind on anything, especially when my tongue's been loosened by the grape.

Excuse me if I blame the wine. Good honest wine, the sort you buy, is cheap, I know, but there are disadvantages to such outstanding discounts. A better wine, even one of modest price, might silence me while I appreciate the smell and flavour or inspect the details on the label. A good wine encourages a little placid introspection. But a bargain wine, in my case anyway, achieves the opposite. It makes me tedious. I am unsettled by the aftertaste. I feel I have to talk to pay you back for asking me, week after week, to share a bottle and some food. This is my only contribution, as you know, because my finances do not allow me to pay you back in other ways. Besides, you look so pained by any silences. I can see it in your eyes; they're darting to and fro, alarmed, demanding that I rescue you by saying something, anything. If I don't talk, you count the lunch a failure. But, if I do all the talking, then I hate myself. And that can't be the proper purpose – or the desired outcome – of a lunch, that your one guest should go away with a lesser opinion of himself and just a little drunker than when he arrived (for I must admit I generally prepare myself for you by stopping off on the way for an aperitif at the Passenger Bar and, occasionally, if we've exhausted our acquaintance more quickly than expected, I console myself on my way home with a digestif there as well).

So here is my proposal. Let's stretch ourselves, expand the pleasures of the lunch, put extra chairs out in the yard. I have a friend whom you would like, a cousin actually, though there does not exist between us any of the reticence that normally you find in families. No, I think you would enjoy our badinage. And he would be a better guest than me, as he is younger and his comments will be fresh. Moreover, he will welcome the attentions of your cats. I have not dared to say before, but I am not a felophile. I do not take exception to the distant view of wildlife in your yard, but I am not happy, let's admit, to have the creatures seeking comfort in my lap or exposing their neat parts below stretched tails as they patrol the table top in search of titbits on our plates.

I'm touched, of course, to see how unselfconscious and indulgent your love of cats can be. But this is something that I trust my cousin is better placed to appreciate than me.

You'd like his wife as well, I think. And she would introduce to your table something that I have missed these last few years, the female outlook on the world. She can express herself most cleverly and in a teasing way that I have never found misjudged or tiresome. Perhaps I ought to implicate you in a secret that might amuse you covertly if we are ever gathered at your table. My cousin's wife and I are ancient friends. She visits me alone. I am, she says, her private rogue. I'm sure you see how she would benefit our lunches.

There is a problem. There always is. My cousin and his wife have greater appetites than us. This is not greed, of course. I am referring to their higher expectations of a meal and their discernment.

I have, you know, been more than happy to settle for the simple compromises that you make with food. A good farm cheese and decent bread, together with a choice of pickles and some fruit, are more than adequate for me. I make my satisfaction clear to you each week by always leaving something untouched on my plate. The fact that sometimes you present me with a cheese that is not fresh that day or with some supermarket bread has never been an issue in my eyes. I know your thoughts. You do not like to see good produce go to waste, no matter that the pickles have been hardened in the sun or the nectarines are bruised and floury. Where would our planet be if food of lesser quality were thrown out? The world would starve.

But, still, you ought to know that my cousin and his wife have wilder tastes. Why would they stir themselves to make the expedition to your ungarnished part of town if they were not beckoned by the prospect of some treats? Do not bankrupt yourself. Some decent pasta would serve well. Or fish. It's always easy to get fish. Our little port sustains more than sixty fishing boats. You'd be surprised by all the choice of species. Equally, the hunting season has begun; it would be simple to lay your hands on some nice game.

I see you wince again. The cooking is too much for you, of course. Well, here's a compromise. If you are short of energy – I sympathize with that, old friend; men of our age cannot be expected to work in kitchens – then there's a way to save your legs and keep your blood pressure down. You are not short of cash, I know. I've seen, by chance, your pension slip. You've worked for over forty years to pay for your retirement and to enjoy an unstinting quality of life. So, now, be generous to yourself. You are deserving of some luxury. Let's put an end to lunches in your yard. It is, anyway, I have to say, a little damp and draughty there. The table and the drains are far too close to each other. I always feel your bread and cheese have just an edge of borrowed pungency. The ripeness I detect is sometimes inappropriate. And, when the instant coffee comes, the smell is blunted, don't you think?

We could move into the house, of course, as we have

done from time to time when it is raining. But it's a little dark in there – and you would be obliged to tidy up if there were guests less liberal than me. No, you should take a taxi to that little restaurant, the Saint Celice, behind my apartment block. Invite the three of us. Four is the perfect number. It is a pity, obviously, that none of us could volunteer to share the burden of the bill. Life's inequalities are always an embarrassment. But I'd be happy to meet you there at any time, as would my cousin and his wife. We are good friends with the proprietor and so you could be certain of a welcome and the grandest meal. Good wine as well. No table cats. Celice is the patron saint of cooks. She graces only the best of kitchens. So, you see, I am proposing something less simple and informal than we have been used to, something less confined at least.

I'll miss your charming yard, of course, but I think we've reached an age when we can be indulgent and immoderate without fear of reproach. We have to change our ways or calcify.

What do you say? We've been having lunch together for so many years. We count on it. It keeps us sane. It would be a pity, don't you think, if our fond custom were to end?

26

Mondazy is the greatest writer from this town, but not the wealthiest. That honour rests with Alicja Leśniak (a pseudonym), who wrote *The Boulevard of Perfect Health* and *The Well of Wellbeing* and sold more than a million copies of each in seven years, not out of bookshops but from cardboard serve-yourself stands inside pharmacies and fitness clubs worldwide. The day after she died, from a stroke in her seventy-first year and not five kilometres from here, the local newspaper attached to its obituary a photograph of Leśniak, looking oddly robust in the driveway of her villa, and the following transcript from one of her famously assertive radio broadcasts:

If you wish to banish migraines from your life avoid the following: champagne, wine and wheat-based alcohol, malt beers, hard cheese (particularly English cheddars and blue varieties), coffee, all forms of chocolate, strong pickles, cigarettes, rhubarb, spinach, tomatoes, cereals, cola, and meats excepting white fish, prawns and chicken breast.

Set a day aside each week for fasting, and an hour every morning for meditation in a screened or darkened room, refreshed only by bottled water, not sparkling. That's a hidden stimulant.

On other days, eat nothing but fruit, preferably pears, before midday, and never drink after your (early) evening meal, except weak tea or water.

Try to include cooked onions or some garlic with every dish. Carrots, too, are generally regarded as safe. Throw sugar, salt and spices in the kitchen bin. They're irritants and, incidentally, ruinous for your complexion. It might be a good idea as well to reduce domestic static by taking your television to the tip and not bothering to renew the radio batteries. Unplug the telephone. A migraine flourishes in noise. Cars and public transport do not help. Nor does a stressful job, nor arguments at home. Do not take over-heated baths. Do not keep pets.

Migraines are occasioned by modern life. Eschew it if you can. Migraines are driven off by purity of spirit. Embrace it if you can. It's best, in all, to live a monkish life, avoid most work except the gentlest, and concentrate on keeping all the pain at bay. You owe it to yourself, no matter what your family or friends might say.

Once you've been clear of migraines for three months, it might be tempting to introduce into your diet one of the foods you've missed the most, but this could cause a more vigorous recurrence of your allergy. It's wiser to be patient and complete the journey until you've truly reached 'the Boulevard of Perfect Health'. You will, of course, have hunger head-aches during this regime, but they shouldn't be confused with migraines, though they might feel just as punishing and last as long.

Within six months, the benefits should start to manifest themselves. Where there was once discomfort, you will now encounter evidence of the kinder and less brutal world ahead. Within nine months your migraines will be vanquished. You'll feel wide-eyed, clear-headed and smooth-browed. Then you'll be calm enough to cope with any pain and strong enough, once in a while, to risk a little coffee or some cheese.

Mondazy, incidentally, wrote in his last year, aged ninety-two, this little *jeu d'esprit* for his great-grandson:

A mi-
graine
is a
certain
sign,
that you
should drink
a case of wine.
Is that confusing?
No, just a lesson
to be learned;
that pain is fine
if it's been earned,
by boozing.

27

I am a pimp of sorts. I have a team of girls. When school is finished and it's low tide, they work for me. I arm them with a bucket and a bag of salt, and send them out on to the flats, between the rock spine and the bar, to hunt for razor clams. They're not paid much, but then the task isn't very difficult. All they have to do is walk barefooted on the rippled sand, on the look-out for the comic, tell-tale squirt of water, which reveals the hiding place. They bend or kneel, peer into the opening of the clam's burrow, drop in a pinch of salt, and wait. No one is sure if it is love or hatred of the salt that makes the clam momentarily protrude its twin valves by half a centimetre and extend its pink and fleshy siphon, as if gasping for light or oxygen, or – given what it most resembles – something lewder.

My girls are quick. They have to seize the brittle upper shell and snap the clam clear of the sand before 'the sea dick' disappears again or, digging with its muscled foot, slides free from their gripping fingers. 'Prick-teasing' is their name for salting clams – though none of them is older than twelve.

Sometimes, between the lunchtime sittings at the restaurant and the early evening customers who come for Sunset Snacks, I sit on the terrace by myself with my binoculars and watch the girls. They have no concentration. In between short bursts of work, I see them kicking loops of sand and water at each other. I see them arguing. I see them playing tag, or writing libels in the sand, or squatting on their haunches, so very far from any bush, to urinate. I have to keep an eye on them. If there's a racing tide or heavy winds I have to call them back. The flats are hazardous. Once in a while, I catch them waving at me from afar. They're out of salt. And then I ride out on the quad bike with a fresh supply. They know I'm watching them.

It is the teacher from their school who bothers me. She's come into the restaurant at night several times, with different men. She loves my clams, however I present them, whether chowdered, steamed with seaweed and a freshener of lemon, grilled with garlic, butter and oregano, tenderized for *zuppa di cannolicchi*, ground up with crumbs and spices and then frittered, or simply boiled and flattered with a sauce. They are, she tells me, 'sweet'. My heart stands still for her when she says 'sweet'.

She also tells me, every time she sees the bill or spots the prices on my menu, that I am exploiting her young pupils, abusing them, that, at the very least, I ought to pay the hunters a quarter of the menu asking price. 'I'll have to organize a strike,' she says.

Last week, she went down with my team when school was closed to try prick-teasing for herself. She splashed along the beach towards the flats just like the rest, bare-footed, her skirt tucked up, her bucket heavy with a half-kilo issue of rough salt. And on her back, a bag of pickings from her kitchen, some sachets of cinnamon and cayenne pepper, tubs of curry powder, twists of jam and pickle in greaseproof paper, a vial of vinegar, packets of sugar and flour, mustard seeds, a bottle of pop. She explained she'd set her girls a project. The usefulness of salt for teasing out clams was, she said, 'unproven'. The pupils had to carry out experiments to understand why clams would pop up so recklessly for salt. Why salt and nothing else, when they were living 'up to their necks' in salt anyway? You might as well hunt rats with air.

I told the teacher how people from the coast had been catching and cooking clams for centuries, and they'd always used salt. It smuggled its flavour into the flesh. They can't all be wrong. 'Indeed they can,' she said. She thought her girls, my team, could prove that a pinch of anything, a drop of anything, was good enough to tease the siphon from its shell. Not just salt would do the trick. She could smuggle other flavours in.

I watched with my binoculars. I watched them bend and kneel and hunt for razor clams with all the products from their teacher's bag. The girls, for once, were working hard. A new project is always fun. They seemed to be more lively on the flats than they had been for weeks. Their buckets, I could tell, were getting full. I could not drag myself away and go to work while they were there. The teacher held me by my brittle shell. I could not take my eyes off her. I would have watched until my eyes were sore, except – too soon – I shamed myself with my binoculars and had to flee, red-faced and fearful, from the terrace. I'd gone too far. I'd caught her squatting on the flats, her skirts held up, her underpants pulled clear, the urine sinking at her feet. The clams for that night's customers were springing up between her legs. And she was beckoning her girls.

She came that evening, of course, to taste her spoils. I shucked and cooked for her, no charge, as payment for her efforts on the beach. I'd not exploit her as I had the girls. She waited in the kitchen, at my side with a beer, while I took my clam knife to her catch, rotating its flat blade between the razor shells to sever the upper muscle. I rinsed the clams clean, showed them to the steam for half a minute and let her eat them on the half-shell, raw. They tasted just like prawns, she said, but not as salty. She liked the satisfying chewiness and swore she could detect the jam, the cinnamon, the pop, and many things besides.

28

Taking down the rucksack in the spring for our first outing, we found the undiscarded detritus of last year's final picnic, the chocolate wrappers and the little thermos flask, the balls of foil that had been used to wrap sandwiches, and a plastic box with half a cake inside, vermilion with age. From deep in the rucksack we retrieved an undiscovered element harder than a curl of tin, which once had been an orange peel, and (looking almost perfect, five months on) a white hen's egg boiled in its shell.

We cracked it open on the window ledge, pulled off its shell, and cut it lengthways into halves. The albumen looked curiously transparent, though edible, despite its age. The yolk was greenish brown and fibrous. The smell was subtle and unnerving.

Our dog would not accept the cake, but she seemed glad to eat the egg. She did not mind the colour or the smell, or care about the months of darkness and neglect. Besides, she liked to see the rucksack and the thermos flask. There'd be a picnic and some exercise at last.

29

Your grandfather was not a modern man. He thought a woman's business was waiting – first on her father, then on her husband, then on their sons – not dressing up in coat and lipstick and going out with friends, like Parisian wives. He made that clear when he was courting me. I found the prospect charming in a way, because I'd loved my father and I wanted sons.

One afternoon – the most shaming day of my life – when we'd been married about ten months and I was hardly pregnant with your eldest aunt, he came back early from the warehouse, wanting to be fed. But I'd gone out with my cousin to the little restaurant, where the pharmacy now is. I'm glad that restaurant has closed. It made me blush to even pass it.

Your grandfather, he tracked me down that afternoon – and naturally he made a dreadful scene, showing off in front of all the women there. You could hear the little coffee spoons rattling on their saucers, he was so loud. I told him why I wasn't in the house when he came home, as quietly as I could, although I trembled as I spoke. My little cousin had called, and we had strolled down to the corner for a conversation and some cake. I wiped my mouth to hide my face from him. There was a smudge of pastry cream reddened by my lipstick on the back of my hand.

Well, as you must have heard from your mother, nothing could silence the man once he'd had a lunchtime drink, particularly on this occasion, with his unexpected audience of captive women, their fingers glued to their coffee cups. He loved an audience of women.

'Am I unreasonable to want her in whenever I come home?' he asked. 'To want her there, to cook for me? To want meals on the table a mere three times a day, like other men? It is the principle. The perfect wife would lay three meals a day on the table even when her husband was not there.'

I pushed my cake and cup away, stood up and, nodding farewell to my cousin, began to walk out of the restaurant. It took too long. He said, 'My wife has dined, I see. Her husband goes without.'

Now that he has died and I am living in the empty house, I have become the perfect wife at last. I am at home for him. I cook my meals and, just for company, lay out an extra, unattended plate, with his wine glass and with a knife and fork wrapped in a napkin, as he liked. Of course, if someone calls, one of our daughters, say, or my pretty niece, then there is already a place set for them at the table. I live in constant hope that even you might come one day. But usually I am alone. I have myself only to serve. I do not tremble. And I do not have to hide my face. These are the joys of widowhood. Again I dine. Again my husband goes without.

30

The rumours started when – a rare event – one of the prison guards was spotted shopping in the square where Jo and his forebears had kept their bakery since 1841. It was the evening before the execution. The next day a murderer was due to die in the correction facility, two kilometres out of town. Too close for comfort. Everybody was on edge. The air seemed thin and aromatic with the prospect and proximity of such a death.

Old baker Jo was bald and staid, and not the most progressive of men. 'Don't waste your sympathy,' he said. But George, his son – the one who runs the bakery today and has become the mirror image of his dad and just as difficult – was a libertarian. He wore long hair tucked up inside his baker's cap, and spent any time when he wasn't slaving for his family in the cake, bread and pastry business at the far end of the quay, with his guitar and some unlikely friends. I used to watch them smoking pot with my binoculars and wish I had the courage to saunter down and join them. He was our only hippie then. And he wore flour in his hair.

It seems the prison guard had drawn attention to himself that evening by buying a suspicious assortment of foods. Some freshly shucked oysters, from the basket girl. Two strawberry milkshakes from the cafeteria. A slab of coffee chocolate. A piece of pummelled beefsteak. Nectarines. It wasn't long before the whispering began. These items had to be the condemned man's final meal, they said. His choices had Death engraved all over them.

Then, of course, when the prison guard was spotted talking to George at the rear door of the shop and money was seen to be exchanged for a bakery bag, any fool could guess what was going on. No doubt about it. The bag contained some of young George's Magic Cookies or Sister Mary Mix or Lebanese Red Loaf or Sweet Dream Biscuits or whatever it was that George provided for those long-haired travellers who queued a touch too patiently each evening amongst the locals waiting for their bread. The murderer, for his last meal, had found a way of dining on oblivion. Good luck to him.

I don't believe that anybody slept too late the following morning. Baker Jo was standing in the street by 8 a.m., affecting an inspection of his window display but really with his eyes fixed on the grey woods high above the town where, at that moment, as they thought, that boy, that man, that murderer was sitting down with plastic plates and plastic cutlery to oysters, milkshake, chocolate, nectarines and beef to fortify his final hour on the earth. He'd save his magic pastries till the last. We all knew that. He'd want to fly away. Surely George's baking, his sorcery, would let the man break free.

The hour struck. Some drivers sounded their horns. An emergency congregation spoke its prayers outside the church. Somebody clapped, but mostly people shook their heads, checked their watches for the umpteenth time, and went about their lives with less than half an eye fixed on the heavens.

I watched the execution through my binoculars from our top room. They pulled the prison buildings into town. I could see the detailed silence of the place, the dead, parked cars, the office doors ajar, the tiny windows of the block, the clouds as solid as the hills. The only movement was a hardly stirring flag. I watched for almost fifteen minutes afterwards. Then the prison came to life again. The yards were quickly filled with exercising men. A van backed up. The winds began to lift the flag and shift the clouds. And, for an instant, I swear, the sky went pink with melody, not death. But I was sentimental in those days. The rumours that I'd heard the evening before had made me ready for, and keen to glimpse, transcendence with a pair of human wings.

George and I have not been friends for many years. I was, I am, too dull for him. But he was unusually friendly when we met at the far end of the quay today. I recalled how I used to spy on him with my binoculars and how I used to wish that we were close. So, while we smoked our cigarettes and looked out across the ocean at the ferries and the tankers, I reminded him of those uncomplicated days. Did he remember how he used to play guitar to foreign girls? He smiled at that. Did he remember those hashish cakes and drug-laced biscuits that he used to bake behind his father's back? He laughed. They'd made him rich. And were they true, those rumours that we heard, about the executed man and what he ate for breakfast?

'That's more than thirty years ago,' George said. 'I can't remember all my customers.' He rubbed his floury hands across the bald crown of his head. The day was loud with wind, and sea, and gulls, the straining of the anchored quay, and, at our backs, the honking cars, the muttered prayers, the clapping hands, the less-than-half-regarded heavens of the town.

'But I'll say this,' George added finally, 'if that guy had my cakes for breakfast, even though it might be thirty years ago, he's flying still. Those cakes of mine were savage stuff. I bet he hasn't even realized he's dead yet. He's giggling up there. He's floating and he's giggling. His pupils are like pinheads. His skull's on fire. He can't stand up. He can't sit down. And, boy, he's hungry. He could eat a horse.'

31

No need to starve. When we were big enough, our parents let us wander in the hills behind the village. We knew the taste of everything – the salty gypsum in the rocks, the peachy flavours in the leaves of morning star, the sulphur of a pigeon's egg boiled in the furnace of the sand. We knew where water was.

Sometimes we begged my uncle for some matches and some cigarettes – to catch scrub fowls. 'Smoke is better than a catapult,' we said. We told him how we'd sit underneath the bushes in the river bed and wait for a donkey or a sheep to come down for the leaves. A goat would do. We'd have to blow smoke from his cigarettes into its ears, and wait for ticks to show themselves in the folds of skin. The grey or blackish ticks weren't any good. We needed one which was red-brown, bloated with sheep or donkey or goat blood. We couldn't grip the tick and twist its jaws free of the skin without its body popping between our fingertips. But, with luck, with one more cigarette, smoke might make it drop free of the ear. We'd have to catch the tick before it hit the ground, or it would burst.

Then it was simple. All we had to do was pull a length of cotton from the bottom of our shirts, lasso the tick and put it on a stone out in the sun, then tie the free end of the cotton to a branch. We'd find a cool place underneath the bush. We wouldn't have to count to ten even before a scrub fowl came. It loved the blood bean of a tick. The captive tick, the cotton line, went down its throat in one. We'd snared our meal.

'We have to be patient,' we told our uncle. 'It can take an hour just to catch our tick. But then it only takes five minutes to trap the bird, and five minutes in the fire to roast it.'

'That must be hard,' he said, 'to catch a donkey or a sheep and then persuade it to stay still while hot smoke tunnels in its ear.'

We shrugged. We laughed. We begged my uncle for his matches and his cigarettes.

It's true, we did sit down below the bushes in the river bed. But we did not care for dining out on scrub fowl. We did not hunt for ticks, or look for sheep and donkeys. We smoked my uncle's cigarettes, one at a time, passing them between us so that the smoke was never idle. 'Smoke is better than a catapult,' we said. We filled our mouths and stomachs up with smoke. We fed on cigarettes. We loved the peach and salt and sulphur in the nicotine, the ashy meat and wood. We waited while our appetites fell free, and hit the stony ground, and burst.

32

The melted fondue cheese was not as tasty as she'd hoped. Her seven friends were only playing with their long-handled forks. They pushed their cubes of bread about inside the *caquelon* with hardly any appetite. She should have used a cooking cheese, or added chunks of blue, or paid the extra for some Gruyère or some Emmental.

The processed cheese that she had favoured had been quick to melt but then had separated over the heat of the tiny, blue-flamed table stove. It had emulsified like sump oil in water. The mixture produced an unappealing greasy skin.

It had been an error, too, to forsake the traditional and generous glug of kirsch in favour of a kitchen wine. What could she do now to save the meal? It must have seemed a good idea – with so much restlessness and irritation at the table – to play a game that no one had heard of, let alone attempted before: strip fondue. Anyone who left a cube of bread in the cheese or dropped a piece before it reached their mouth would have to pay the forfeit of removing an item of clothing.

Hot cheese is famous for its treachery. It is a law unto itself. Its strings and globules have scant regard for the principles of adhesion. It worships gravity. A long-handled fork and a shaking hand are no match for it.

It was not long, therefore, before her company of friends was getting naked at the table. It was not long, either, before the scorching cheese was dropping on to unprotected flesh. Her pretty colleague from the office was the first to suffer. Her knee received a nasty, clinging burn. The men on either side of her were quick to cool the knee down with napkins dampened with Perrier. Another of the men suffered a lesser burn across his chest, but it was difficult to remove the stiffening cheese from his hair. His girlfriend tried to flick it off with her long fork and only partially succeeded. But then another woman, not known for her discretion, made a better job of cleaning him up with her fingers and her teeth. It now became a secondary rule of strip fondue that mislaid cheese could not be retrieved by the person who had dropped it.

Quite soon her friends were dropping cubes of cheese-soaked bread into their laps. Almost wilfully, you might have thought. A gasp of pain. The whiff of sizzling flesh and hair and cheese. The welcome offer of the fork, or the fingers, or the teeth.

By the time all the cheese had gone, nobody at the table was without a burn and a poultice of damp napkin. Even those who had been reluctant at first to lose as much as their socks and risk a scorching had in the end decided this was not a dish to miss. Everybody produced at least one set of welts and blisters to nurse as they drove home.

Next day, if anybody asked, 'What did you do last night?' or, 'How was the meal round at your friend's?', how many of the guests would have the nerve to pull their jumpers up or tug their trousers down to show and justify their scars? Here was something to keep quiet about. It would, though, be tempting to repeat the meal with other friends, to suffer at the ends of forks again, to bare themselves before the scorching treachery of cheese, and hope for fresh disfigurements.

33

They spoiled the little beach house, fitting new window frames, daubing paint on ancient, silvered wood, cutting back the creeper, adding a veranda, and putting up a perspex barrier to keep, they said, the sand away but save the fine views of the sea. Old Mrs Schunn would be turning in her grave if she'd lived to see these changes to her home. She wouldn't like the way they disinfected everything as if the place were full of dirt and germs.

Perhaps that's why – respect for her, revenge – I failed to warn them that where they'd put their iron bench and table was also where, every couple of years, the toilet waste was buried from the house's ninety-litre barrel. But anyone with half a nose and a quarter coffee spoon of brains should have recognized the salty, oceanic smell of latrine earth and kept away. Perhaps they thought it was the sea.

They'd picked the garden's only green and pretty spot

for their retreat. Despite the covering of seaweed and sand, our neighbour's hidden night-soil provided nourishing, warm loam for plants.

I should have warned them also, I guess, about the fruits and vegetables that flourished there. These volunteers had not been planted from the packet. But, by the time the summer came and seeds processed by Mrs Schunn's large and active bowel had produced three verdant, aromatic melons and a healthy patch of tomatoes, I was too amused and irritated by the newcomers to intervene.

They'd speed down on Friday nights in their grand car, sit out with their iced drinks amongst their plants and watch the sun set through the perspex barrier. I'd see them picking their tomatoes from the stem and eating them like kids with sweets. They'd never tasted finer toms, it seemed.

They called me over for a drink on the day they harvested their melons. They sliced one open for themselves, squeezed a lemon over it, and powdered it with nutmeg. I said how sweet it smelled. My private joke. And so they offered me a melon, to take home. That might have been the time to tell the truth.

I have not dared taste my melon yet. Though that's not logical, I know. All fruits and vegetables benefit from manure. But Mrs Schunn had been our neighbour for almost twenty years. We knew her far too well to take a knife to her or eat the products of her waste. Yet I might dry and save the seeds for the coming season. It seems the least that I can do. Respect for her and for her disfigured house.

So the melon darkens, softens, ages on my window

shelf. The raised embroidery that nets the skin is losing its rigidity. There is a bluish mould around the puncture of the stem scar. The sap is leaking from a split. Already I can trace the brackish odour of decay.

34

Whenever she ate fish, her eyes puffed up and watered, her nostrils closed, the tissues of her mouth and throat rose like dough, damp and squashy, until she had to gawp for breath, just like a bruised and netted cod, tossed on the deck. Her skin became as mottled as cheap veal and her heart metamorphosed into a moth, flapping and scorching itself against the fevers of her ribcage. The symptoms were not fatal in a woman of her size – though sometimes children died of toxic shock from eating fish – but, obviously, she did her best to avoid seafood, to check a menu carefully, to study the ingredients of any can, to mistrust relishes and pastes, to make sure that anyone who asked her home to eat was warned well in advance. It was nine years since she'd collapsed so comically at the Cargo Restaurant in front of all her colleagues. She hadn't realized the soup had fish in it until, before the entrée arrived, she'd flushed and paled and slipped down off her chair as if her bones had suddenly dropped into her shoes, as if she had been filleted.

So when she didn't want to turn up at her sister's funeral, would rather die than show her face, would rather swell to twice her size than add her small voice to the hymns, she bought herself a piece of fish for supper – two fillets of blue-water mackerel. She had them decapitated, boned and skinned in the shop. Disguised, in fact, so that she wouldn't gag at just the sight of them. Her uncooked meal looked more like mozzarella than fish.

The flesh was yellowish and pungent in the dish – that lewd and acrid smell of fin and brine – but still it did not seem particularly hazardous. She pasted the fillets with mustard, sprinkled them with salt, baked them for half an hour, ate them in her armchair with a fresh brunette of bread, and fell asleep.

Next morning, after a night of storm-tossed dreams and nausea, she was, as she'd expected, at death's door, scarcely strong enough to lean across from the armchair to reach the telephone. Her fingers were like woollen sausages. Her lungs were sponge. Her hot and cold sensations had reversed, so that although her hands were scorching the inside of her mouth was dry and wintry. Her lips were tingling at first, then numb. She phoned her brother's house. She couldn't come, she told him, not with the best will in the world. She was too weak and too distressed. Her face was twice its normal size. If only he could see how weak she was, how mournful.

He couldn't see, but he could hear. His sister's voice was muffled, breathless, tense. She'd have to have the benefit of his doubt.

That afternoon, after the interment, the brother and three other mourners visited her, with flowers and some fruit and a printed copy of the church service. They caught her sitting in the same armchair where she had slept, a box of tissues on her lap. Her eyes were pools of tears. Her nose was streaming and her lungs were drowned. They'd never seen her so beleaguered. They'd never seen a woman so distressed, so changed and damaged by her grief. To tell the truth, they felt ashamed to be so calm and well themselves, to be so full and scrubbed and smart while she was so reduced.

She begged them not to worry. She'd be well. She'd only got a bug, some passing thing. They ought to let her sleep in peace and, in a day or two, she'd phone to say she had recovered and could begin to come to terms with her great loss.

35

On birthdays in our village on the estuary, where spitting was as commonplace as fish, we had a sweet observance for the children. We didn't blow out candles on the cake. Instead, once we had finished feasting at the trestles under the tarbony trees, we spat the past year out, its disappointments and its failures, the lies we'd told, our arguments, our cruelties. We expectorated all our vices, errors and misdeeds so that our coming year could start anew.

All you needed was a bunch of grapes. With the neighbours and the family gathered round, your classmates, your parents' friends, you'd have to eat one grape for every year of your life. You had to burst and eat the flesh but save the pips. Quite difficult. To swallow one would be to swallow last year's wickedness. You'd tuck the pips into a corner of your mouth or push them up into the space between your top teeth and your lip. A two-year-old – and so a child relatively free from sin – would only have

to store, say, seven pips in its soft mouth. A boy of fifteen
– a scamp, a self-abuser and a stop-abed, as you'd expect –
would have to tuck away, say, thirty pips or more. There
was, of course, a lot of laughter and some tickling to make
the task more difficult.

By the time you'd eaten your last grape, the birthday
guests would have formed a circle, and would be moving,
hand in hand, around the birthday child. There'd be a
countdown – ten, nine, eight . . . And on the shout of 'Go!'
you'd have to spit out all your pips. You'd spray the
dancing circle with your flinty, salivating sins. It was a
blessing and an honour to be hit. Ours was, as I have said,
a village used to spitting and used as well to sending all its
faults and its offences into the past.

It is, in fact, my twenty-seventh birthday today. I do not
have the courage to phone home. I'm going out with
friends tonight to celebrate. But in the hours I had to kill
this afternoon I went down to the market streets far below
my small apartment to treat myself. A book, the latest
Bosse CD and a bunch of local grapes. Black grapes. In
these supermarket days those are the only ones with any
pips.

Like almost every guilty man who has neglected home
and family, I am a sentimentalist. I placed the CD on the
stereo, selected its romantic track. I burst my twenty-seven
homesick grapes between my teeth and stored the almost
sixty pips against the soft side of my mouth. Of course, I
had no dancing witnesses. I counted down from ten to
one myself, silently, hardly daring to move my lips. Then,
standing at the open window, I threw back my head and

spat my disappointments out into the street. Before I had the chance to look, I heard the clatter of my twenty-seven birthdays strike the windscreens and the roofs of passing cars. In that same instant, I glimpsed a shaded stretch of water far beyond the town, a stand of trees, abandoned tables, and the turning circle of my half-remembered friends, smiling, smiling, but with no one at their centre from whom to take the impact of those past forgiven years.

36

There is no greater pleasure than to be expected at a meal and not arrive.

While the first guests were standing in the villa's lobby with their wet hair and their dry wine, their early efforts at a conversation saved and threatened by fresh arrivals at the door, he was driving slowly in the rain along the coastal highway, enjoying his loud absence from the room, enjoying first the cranes and depots of the port, and then the latest condominiums, the half-glimpsed by-passed villages with their dead roads, the banks of coastal gravel, the wind, the darkness and the trees.

While they were being seated at the dining table and were thinking – those who knew him – Lui's always late, he was taking pleasure from the water on the tarmac, the old movie romance of the windscreen wipers and the dashboard lights, the prospect of the speedy, starless, hungry night ahead.

At what point would his sister, or her husband George, dial his home (discreetly from another room) to get only the answerphone and leave the message . . . What? Was he OK? Had he forgotten that they'd asked him round to eat with friends? Would he come late? Was he aware what trouble he'd put them to? Would he arrive in time to charm the sweet young teacher that they'd found and placed at his left elbow?

At what point would his plate, his napkin and his cutlery be gathered up and two women be asked to shift their chairs along to fill his place and break the gendered pattern at the table?

At what point would his hostess say 'It's not like him at all'?

While they were eating in his absence – a sweetcorn soup, a choice of paddock lamb or vegetarian risotto, Mother Flimsy's tart with brandy – he was driving with one hand and, with the other, breaking pieces off his chocolate bar. He was dreaming repartee and dreaming manners of a king, and being far the smartest, sharpest person in the room.

While they were sitting in his sister's long salon, for coffee and a little nip of Boulevard Liqueur, and getting cross about some small remark their host had made at their expense, Lui reached the hundred-kilometre mark that he had set himself. He took the exit from the highway, slowed down to drive the narrow underpass – sixty sobering metres of bright lights, dry road, wind-corralled litter, a couple sheltering – and turned on to the opposite lane. He headed back towards the town and home, another hundred k, a hundred k less cinematic, less romantic, and more futile than the journey out.

The rain, now coming from the right, presented unexpected angles for the car. It tilted at the windscreen with more percussion than before. He had to put his wipers on their fastest setting. The smell was weather, chocolate, gasoline. The skyline warmed and lifted with its fast-advancing lights, those attic rooms, those bars, those streets, those television sets, those sweeping cars and cabs, those marriages that brighten up the night.

His eyes were sore and tired. His mouth was dry. He'd have to concentrate to take his pleasure from the drive, his safe and happy absence from the room, his prudent, timid, well-earned thirst. He put a steady glass up to his lips and sipped. Dipped his spoon into the sweetcorn soup. Chose the lamb. Nodded at the windscreen wipers for a second helping of the tart. How witty he could be, how certain in his views, how helpful with the wine, how neat and promising. The pretty woman on his left extended her slim arm and squeezed his hand by way of thanks for his good company, and slipped out of the room into his car, a passenger, an absentee, the gender pattern at the table restored. He broke his chocolate bar in half and shared with her the unfed, midnight journey into town.

37

He kept a curved plate in the middle of his kitchen table, with carvings on its edge. The sun, the moon, some leaves, some stars. It wasn't old or valuable, but it was natural wood, unvarnished and hand-decorated. Each day, first thing, once he had done his lifts and bends, he placed his titbits on the plate, food to see off death. Pumpkin seeds to protect the prostate. Bran for bowels. Brazil nuts for their selenium. Dried apricots. French pitted prunes. Linseed. A tomato. There were no supplements or vitamins. He had no confidence in pills. Then he drank his green leaf tea with honey from the comb. He was a regimented man, well-organized, reliable. He kept his diet up, without a break, until the day he died.

38

One summer holiday, when I was nine or thereabouts, living in the blocks behind the port, my mother got me out from underneath her feet by setting up a game of pass the cake. It was, she promised me, a way of finding out what kind of neighbour, wife and cook I'd be when I grew up, and also a lesson in The Expansion of Good Deeds.

The proper way to pass the cake, she said (making me write down her instructions) was this: on Friday, I should pour a single cup containing sugar, milk and flour into a covered bowl, take it down with me into the yard and whistle for my gang of girls. We'd have to find a secret place, away from cats and rats and boys, to hide the bowl. On Saturday, all the girls should gather round and take their turn at stirring the mixture and making a wish.

Sunday was the day of rest, so we'd do nothing to the bowl all day, except to say a prayer for it: 'Dear God, don't let the boys sniff out our cake.' On Monday, I would have to add another cup of sugar, milk and flour; on Tuesday, everybody should stir the mixture, make a wish again; on Wednesday, yet another cup from me; on Thursday, stir and wish a final time.

When the second Friday came around, it would be my honour to remove two cups of mixture from my bowl and give them to two friends to start their own cakes, to add and stir and mix with help from all of us throughout the following week. 'One cake, you see, produces two.'

Once my cake had given birth to twins, my mother said, I could take what I had left inside my bowl, and come upstairs to see what she had to spare, an egg, some oil, some apple and sultanas, perhaps, or the last jam in the jar. And once I'd mixed these extras in – so long as I did not clutter up the kitchen for too long – I could bake my cake in the family oven. Then all I had to do was eat it up on Saturday, outside, sharing it with the girls and looking forward to sharing theirs in all the weeks ahead.

If everybody played their part and kept their faith, then my cake would have produced four unbaked grandchildren by the following Friday, mother explained, jotting down the figures underneath the recipe, eight unbaked great-grandchildren within the fortnight, and 1,024 fully cooked descendants within twelve weeks of the game starting. 'Before the year is up that little cup of sugar, milk and flour will have fed the world,' she said, pushing me towards the door. I was content to let her rest while I ran down to the gang with my astounding bowl.

That was the proper way to pass the cake. But, when you're nine or thereabouts, a week is an eternity. We could not wait. We sat, the dozen in our gang, out in the stairwell with our bowls and her instructions, and bred our future generations in an afternoon. At one o'clock we put my starting cup of sugar, milk and flour in my bowl. At five past one we stirred and wished. By one thirty-five, we'd filled two more bowls, our eldest twins, and were already cooking the first cake. In less than six hours, by our reckoning, we would have made 10,000 wishes, offered up a multitude of prayers, and passed the cake into every household in the Blocks. We would, indeed, have fed the world within the two weeks of our holidays, we would have made the generations hunger-free, if there had been (there never are) sufficient girls and bowls.

39

Here is his name, written in our register the day before he died: Toby Erickson, in capitals, above his signature, his home address (illegible), his phone number, his fax. He'd come to stay for four nights, for the angling. He seemed polite and well-to-do and not unsettled by his own company or by the dumbing prospects of the sea.

On the first morning – a beryl sky, with hardly any wind – he phoned down to our jetty house to hire a motor boat and a set of sea rods with some bait. He planned to anchor out in the drift stream, amongst the floods of migrating fish. He'd set his heart, he said, on catching tad. Not easy with a hook and line. A friend of his – and one he needed to impress – would dine with him that evening, so could we cook the tads he caught? Of course we could, we said. Our chef's a genius with fish. 'Good angling, Mr Erickson. We have prepared a packed lunch for your trip.'

Here are his signatures again – the boatman's log,

insurance forms, acknowledgements that he had read the boat-hire safety file. This listed all the dangers and the protocols: fouling the propellers in the wrack, being pushed on to the west side of the low-tide buoys, using emergency flares, always wearing a safety line and a buoyancy suit, giving way to sail, staying within clear sight of the hotel. 'Remember: Our seas are prone to sudden swells,' it warned in red. It's a pity no one thought to caution him about the lunch.

Here is the list of foodstuffs in our 'Gourmet Picnic Lunch for Anglers'. It is a feast: one cold-meat baguette with *cornichons*, rye slices from the bakery, a Baby Camembert, a casket of salad vegetables, fresh seasonal fruit, a choice of home-baked mini-pastries, Swiss chocolate, a flask of filter coffee (select from Java / Harrar / mocha) or hot water with infusions, a half of our House White, your pick of bottled beers. Who'd think that there were any hazards there?

The boatman checked on Mr Erickson with his binoculars throughout the day. There was, he says, a pancake sea and barely a cloud, so nothing to cause concern. The boat was anchored on the clear side of the wrack with its outboard lifted and correctly tucked. Three fixed rods had been deployed. The gentleman was sitting midships, wearing his yellow buoyancy suit and a straw hat. It was the warmest, stillest day for weeks and not especially good for catching tad. The tad likes choppy seas and hates harsh light. The boatman judged it was the safest afternoon for him to leave his post and drive down to the town 'for business and a drink'.

The friend arrived a little after seven in the evening and

took her aperitif out on to the terrace to wait for the fishing boat to lift its anchor and come home. We joked with her. 'He'll not return, your friend, until he's caught his tad for dinner.' Here is the bar chit that she set against his room. And here's her signature.

Nobody noticed when the woman gave up hope and left. And nobody noticed, as the dark set in, that Mr Toby Erickson was still at sea. This is a busy place at night. Chef had more than fifty covers to cook for. And all the hotel's rooms were booked.

Next morning, the boatman went out in the launch with our manager to bring the body in. It was a little choppier, a better day for catching fish. Our guest was still sitting midships, stiff as wood. He'd caught his tad that night, but hadn't had the chance to play it in and lift it off the hook. An open bottle had spilled beer on to the deck. What remained of the 'Gourmet Picnic Lunch for Anglers' was being picked clean by gulls. The rescue flare had been unpacked from its holdings but had not been fired. There was evidence – again picked clean by gulls – of vomiting. It seemed his death had not been swift. We guessed – incorrectly – he'd had a heart attack or stroke.

We have a protocol: a hotel has at least one death a year. There is a laundry room which can be used for corpses. They had to dislocate his shoulder blade to get the buoyancy suit off so that he was presentable. His face was yellow. Like the suit. The police were called. Somebody phoned the contact number that he'd written in the register to give the sad news to the stranger at the other end.

*

How did he die? Just when? There are no documents to say. But once the magistrates had finished their reports, and diagnostic tests had been returned from the laboratories, the agent of his death was named. The culprit was a home-baked mini-pastry, which chef had filled with country-canned asparagus. Low-acid vegetables that have been canned by amateurs at room temperature, it seems, are rich in vitamins and poisons. Under such conditions poisons multiply. Here is the Chemical Analysis, which shows that Mr Erickson's mini-pastry – and the remaining contents of the can – was rich enough in the neuro-toxin *Clostridium botulinum* to slay a team of horses. He would have found his vision blurred at first. He'd be dry-mouthed, a little weak. Nothing to panic about. He'd blame it on the gently rocking boat. He might have dozed and, when he woke, felt stiff and rheumatoid – first signs of his paralysis, the clamping of his lungs, his loss of reflex and the wrenching pain. If only chef had made another fifty little pies, he could have put a corpse in every room.

Here is a picture difficult to banish from our minds. It's gone midnight. The moon and stars are bearing down on the anchored boat. Our Toby Erickson is dead. He sits quite still, in his straw hat, intoxicated, and untroubled by the nagging sea. His first and final tad – the dinner catch that might impress his lady friend – is hooked and tugging on the deep end of his line. It can't escape from predators. The carnivores will pick it clean before the night is done. The bones above the water are holding on to bones below. The numb are fishing for the numb.

At last, his boat is shifting slightly on its ropes as tides regress and winds align in readiness for the day. The hotel staff are innocent, as yet. They are preparing breakfasts for their guests, unscrewing pots, opening cans, cutting off the tops of cartons, snipping sachets, breaching packets, breaking eggs, and quietly laying out the feast.

40

Our concierge has been away. A short break from sitting in other people's draughts for a living, she explains. She's spent a week at Anderbac Falls, where she went on her vacations as a child. She's come back with the benefits burned on her face. The weather was fabulous, the Falls miraculously unchanged in all those years, and to top it all she's forged what might prove to be a lasting friendship with a man. 'A widower,' she adds. The word – she almost whispers it – bestows decorum, as if his marriage and bereavement put this new liaison beyond reproach. So, nothing like the noisy, inappropriate affair she's been conducting with the janitor – 'a bachelor' – in his apartment on the seventh floor.

Her widower is charming and presentable, she explains, well-read, well-heeled, well-dressed, though somewhat overweight. And he is kind. 'I'm torn up over him.' They'd picnicked together in the woods, had shared a table at a restaurant, and on their final night together had jointly cooked a meal in the little chalet which he'd been renting in the grounds of her hotel.

'He never tried to touch me even once, you know,' she says, to illustrate how genuine her new suitor had proved himself to be. 'Though if he'd tried he might have found me willing. I'd drunk a half a bottle of his wine. And he was so respectable – and such a cook! – that I would have liked to show my gratitude. But still he said his wife was present in the room. They'd rented that same chalet the year before she died. He said that I was sitting in her chair.'

You have to interrupt the concierge. If you don't, she'll wrap you up in conversation until (my mother's phrase) your bladder turns to stone. Before you realize it the taxi driver's tired of waiting, or the shop has closed, or your appointment has been missed, or the slow stew you've left to cook upstairs has been reduced to clinker, ash and smoke. And so I have to turn towards the street and say, 'I'll catch up with the details when I get back, but now I really have to go.'

I've looked down at my watch and pulled a face. I've said 'Oh, dear . . .' to show how late I am. Already I have reached the double door, but I feel as if I've been too hurried, impolite. I turn and add 'Well, good for you . . .' and then, once I'm halfway down the steps and have almost broken free, 'I'm stopping off at George's tonight, if you want anything . . .'

'Why not? I owe myself a little treat. Can you bring two cheese pies? And if he has those baby macaroons, then six.'

*

I almost get back to the block this evening without her cheese pies and her macaroons. It's been an awkward day, too argumentative, too rushed. My head's a sieve. I don't need shopping for myself. There's cold meat in the fridge to finish off and then I'd like to curl up in my bed and sleep. It's not until I reach the baking smell that I remember our concierge's 'little treat'. I get the taxi driver to circle the square and wait for me at George's. The driver hands me some change and asks me to bring him 'something hot'. Nobody can be downwind of George's and not want food.

I think that I'm in luck. The concierge is not behind her desk. But by the time I've pushed her bag of food beneath the metal grille, she's at my side. We used to have a little dog called Plum, before my husband left. Just like the concierge. You couldn't move, you couldn't sneak yourself a tiny piece of cake, you couldn't slip out of the house, without the dog appearing at your side.

The concierge is keen to carry on where we left off. 'My widower could outbake George,' she says. A little romance suits her well. I see she's had her hair in curlers and changed out of her 'mopping slacks' into her going-out dress. It's no longer difficult to picture her in an Anderbac restaurant, across the table from an attentive man.

I say, 'Excuse me if I hurry off. My head's on fire . . .' Already I have reached the elevator door.

'Hold on for me,' she says. 'I'm coming up.' This is a pretext, I am sure, for pursuing our conversation. But I'm resigned to her, and oddly touched, despite my throbbing head. For it is touching when a woman of her age finds this late blessing in her life.

And so I have to wait five minutes with my foot holding the door until she joins me in the elevator, with her keys and carry bag.

'When will you have the chance to see this man again?' I ask.

'Next year,' she says.

'Next year?'

'Same week, same place.'

'You might not like him in a year.'

'That doesn't worry me. We both like the falls at Anderbac and they won't change. We thought it would be safest if we met up there again. A year soon goes. We'll write. We'll phone. We're not young kids. If you're attracted to a man at my age, then what's the hurry? It'll be something to look forward to. What do they say? It's better to travel than arrive.'

At last she pulls shut the elevator door and I can head towards my room, my cold meat supper and my bed.

'What floor?' I ask, my finger hovering above the ten buttons of the console.

She smiles. I think that beneath the suntan and the make-up she almost blushes. 'The seventh floor,' she says. She bites her lower lip – there's lipstick on her teeth – and looks down at her shoes.

It's not until we reach the janitor's floor – and his two dogs are already barking at his door in greeting – that she confides in me. She's backing out into the hall, into the early evening smell of other people's meals, pushing the elevator door with her bottom. She opens up her carry bag to let me see inside. A bottle of wine. The paper packet full of treats that I have brought from George's: two pies, six baby macaroons.

'You spoil that man,' I say.

'Well, yes, perhaps I do. Perhaps I shouldn't be so cheap. A macaroon's too good for him.' She tips her head towards the undeserving janitor, towards his raucous dogs. 'You wouldn't say this one's well-read, well-dressed, well-heeled! You wouldn't say this one won't try to get his hands on me.' She backs away into the dark. 'But, still, a woman's got to eat if she's to keep herself in trim. And no one wants to eat alone, not when your heart's torn up like mine.'

41

Spitting in the omelette is a fine revenge. Or overloading it with pepper. But take care not to masturbate into the mix, as someone in the next village did, sixty years ago. The eggs got pregnant. When he heated them they grew and grew, becoming quick and lumpy, until they could outwit him (and all his hungry guests waiting with beer and bread out in the yard) by leaping from the pan with their half-wings and running down the lane like boys.

42

This was the challenge that they faced. To cook their meal without a cooker or a pot. The boys had brought their tents out to the island in the stream for just three nights of liberty. It had been heavy work, toiling up the valley with their gear. They had their sleeping bags, their cartons of packaged, tinned and foil-wrapped food, their plastic plates and cutlery, their gas bottle.

But someone – let's not spoil their weekend yet by naming names – had failed to put the little cooker and the pots and pans into his bag. It didn't matter on day one. They ate the fruit, the biscuits and the bread, the chocolate, the cereal. That night they made a fire – at least the boy we should not name had packed the matches – and dined on toast and jam. Next morning they ate the bacon and the meat goujons, roasted on a flat stone in the fire. Their lips were singed and ashy. They drove away the taste with candy bars.

By the evening of day two they were immensely hungry, bored as well. They had misjudged their rations. All that remained to eat were eggs and rice. The boys knew that it was possible to fry an egg on the bonnet of a 1950s car. They'd seen a photograph – a silver Buick, four spitting eggs, sunny side up, the bluest sky, the baking hills of Stovepipe Wells in California. But this was not America, nor was it warm, nor were there any cars. If only they could find an old tin can, then they could boil their supper. But this was untouched countryside. The sort of people who liked this kind of landscape did not leave their trash behind.

At first they thought these deprivations would be fun. They'd have to hunt for food, catch fish, like cavemen, cook their conquests on an open fire. But there were no fishing rods or nets. There were no traps or snares. There was no wildlife other than themselves, as far as they could tell.

The only option, then, was to find some way to boil their eggs without a pot or pan. It could be done. It had been done, so many times, 4,000 years before. Their island was an ancient place, a proven refuge for the night, where hunters, travellers might camp in those far days before the larder and the fridge. If those ancestors had some eggs, then they'd not have to wait until a Buick limousine turned up. All they'd have to do was dig a hole and line it with clay from the river bank, then fill it with water carried in skins. A constant supply of red-hot stones baked in their fire would make the water tumble-boil and cook the eggs to perfection. Indeed, the challenge could be met quite readily, but not by boys who hadn't studied their pre-history.

So they sat round the fire that second night and contemplated something worse than hunger. They contemplated river, night and clay, the broken landscape and the perfect eggs, the foolishness of camping by this unceasing and unfeeding stream. They dreamed of being more courageous than they were, of being braver boys. And when the rain began to fall they contemplated their defeat of going home as soon as it was light, a whole day earlier than planned, and smuggling back that box of eggs into the simpler, chilling, less historic place from which they'd taken it.

43

There was an eating contest after the bride had left with her new husband on their honeymoon and all the duller couples had gone upstairs to their expensive rooms to sleep off the excesses of the day. Just nine men remained amid the debris of the dancing and the meal – five of the younger and more hearty guests, reluctant to bring such an amusing, colourless event to an end, the Spanish barman, two waiters and the hotel's under-manager (who clearly wanted everyone to go to bed). All bachelors, all dressed (approximately) in white. That was the wedding theme. All white. A vulgar, wealthy man can have exactly what he wants when his youngest daughter marries, and this one wanted everything and everybody white. That meant a brand-new carpet in the hotel's dining room, redecorated walls and doors, pearl tablecloths (hand-stitched with hearts in matching thread), displays of the very palest roses, lilies and carnations, and, of course, a wedding dinner 'cooked from white ingredients'. An irritating challenge for the hotel's chef.

The day had been exciting and bizarre. The ninety guests arrived to find themselves blanched out by lighting from the chandeliers and by the artificial snow heaped up in all the corners of the rooms. They must have felt they'd stepped on to the set of a television advertisement for heaven or into some uncanny alpine hospital. Perhaps that's why they drank and laughed so heartily. They felt such fools. But, when the waiters in their white smocks arrived to load the tables with the food, they had to clap. The chef had achieved the impossible. They sat at their appointed places and reverently picked their ways through fourteen spotless dishes, which seemed less vivid even than the chalky china tableware from which they had been served.

It was the barman's fault. He said it was a pity that the waiters had to waste good drinking time clearing up the mess. It was a pity, too, that such eccentric food should go to waste. 'Let's eat the lot,' he said. 'I bet we can.'

'In less than twenty minutes,' said the under-manager, 'or else you lose the bet. I want you out by two.'

The nine of them, keyed up and challenged by the errant spirit of the wedding night, spread out around the tables and set to work on what remained of the feast. There were no rules or etiquette, no social niceties. So lung and lychees shared a fork; fish steaks and sallow *andouillettes* were sweetened by the icing from the wedding cake; baby white aubergines and boiled potatoes were dipped into the coconut sauce; prawn crackers scooped up basmati rice, yoghurt dip and cream. The men made sandwiches of white oat bread, buffalo cheese, blanched asparagus and stiffened albumen. Vanilla ice cream went with everything. Speed was the thing. This was a race against the clock. They had to cram their mouths. If anything fell on the carpet, then so what? It didn't show. By the time – eighteen minutes – everything had been dispatched, their suits, shirts and trousers were spattered with niveous gravies and with grease, white stains on white.

They filled their glasses with the last dregs from the bottles of white wine, mixed drunkenly with milk, and held them up to toast the bridegroom and the bride, by now a hundred miles away. The bachelors could only picture them and hope their own white day would come, their own fake snow. Somewhere, driving through the night, the honeymooners were in each other's arms, his lips on hers, deep in the lambswool cushions of their white limousine, behind the stiff and blushing chauffeur in his pallid uniform.

44

Beware the chilling phrase 'This calls for some champagne!' Resist that weighty bottle if you can. Champagne will spoil the day.

Champagne is tolerable at times, equal to a glass of lemonade for sweetening dry throats, superior even to a can of beer for brisk inebriation, preferable to home-made wine or cider. But otherwise obey the warning on the label: 'Open with care.' The drink is rarely equal to its task or to its reputation. How could it be? Nothing is that heavenly or transcendent. We should hold champagne in contempt. It lets us down.

I have collected two bottles of Moët & Chandon, Brut Impérial, from the cold pantry, to celebrate my husband's success at work. The Director at last. Bravo! I carry them like liquid luck down to the summer house. His mother's there, three colleagues, his two best friends, our daughter and her current partner, a neighbour and (reluctantly) his wife. With us that's twelve. One bottle wouldn't be enough. It wouldn't be enough to spoil the day.

What – apart from my husband – could be more well-mannered and more sociable than two bottles of champagne? Placed at the centre of the trellis table, they strike, like him, a solid attitude. They're dignified. But they're light in disposition, smartly presented, aspiring. Their pedigrees are on display. Their rising gases promise both energy and levity. Expense has not been spared.

My husband likes to open bottles of champagne himself. He feels I lack respect. The bubbly is too finely and too patiently blended, too lovingly matured to handle with anything other than finesse, he says. We should not allow a pressure spill to waste any. He stands at his end of the table, tears back the gold, loosens the wire and shows us how to pull and twist the cork. The finest waiter could not better him. A flying cork might add some drama but is, in his opinion, unnecessary and vulgar. Everybody laughs and sighs at the muted popping of the corks, the barest frothing of the champagne.

We hold our glasses out and watch the tumbling liquid and the fizz. We lift our glasses. Trembling hands. We have to drink at once. The bubble reputation will not last. Our disappointments and our jealousies will soon be heavy in the glass.

'Congratulations,' someone says. 'To your success.'

We all stand up to toast my husband and his good fortune. He has a smile for everyone. He would not understand how chilled we feel and vexed. He's sparkling now. He is *grand cru*. He does not know that he has let us down.

45

The celebrated restaurant is a short walk from the transport stores, westwards, towards the empty tenements. Just ask the way if you get lost or muddled in the yards and alleyways. A magazine article – with the headline 'Simply the Best' – has said it serves the finest soup in the region and 'merits the detour'. So, for a month or two, its tables are reserved by detourists, as we call them, and regulars like the Fiat garage workers and the women from the trade exchange must eat elsewhere.

The menu is a simple one. It has not changed for seven years at least and will not change until she dies, the owner says. Each diner gets a hock of bread, some butter and some salt, a spoon, an ashtray and a glass. There are sometimes three soups to choose from. One made with fish, of course. The port is nearby and fish is plentiful. Another's made with vegetables, according to the season. And, occasionally, there is a third, prepared from either beef or chicken. But most days there are only two, fish soup or vegetable. A glass of beer or water is included in the price. There is no point in asking for an omelette or some wine. The restaurant can't cope with such variety. The best you'll get is soup and beer and smoke. There's also little point in asking what the fish is for that day, or what fresh vegetables were used. The owner usually says, 'You'll have to wait and see', because, to tell the truth, she's not entirely sure.

You could not say the place is celebrated for its ambience. It's just a corner house converted forty years ago into a lunchery, at a time when there were countless families living in this quarter of the town and employed in the naval joineries and engineering shops. It's modest, then, and not entirely clean. It's two rooms up and one room down, with plastic tablecloths and kitchen chairs to make you feel at home. It's cheap in there and cramped and, unusually for a celebrated restaurant these days, it's heavy with tobacco smoke.

If not the ambience, then what? You find out when you lift the soup spoon to your lips. The soups are never liquidized into a smooth consistency but, even with their nuggets and morsels of flesh and vegetable, the substrate ballast of lentils, peas and beans, the broth is so delicate and light, so insubstantial and so resonant, that taste and smell precede the near lip of the spoon and leap across the thin air to your mouth. You've heard of aftertaste? This is the opposite. This is a soup that's full of promises. We're not surprised. We're used to it.

These detourists, however, are perplexed as they depart between the crowded tables and step out through the narrow door into the diesel-smelling streets. They tip like kings and queens. Their tips are stiffer than the bill. It can't be right, they think, to dine so well and simply and be so cheaply satisfied. And, oh, such soup, such soup! The magazine has said the owner has a secret formula, an additive she will not name. So now they try to guess what they have tasted, other than the finest recipe not only in the region but in the world. What is the conjuring trick?

We have the answers, should they ask. When we have drunk a beer or two, then we will gladly tease the cook, the celebrated chef, with theories to explain the new-found eminence of her restaurant. Her secret is the sewer truffles that she adds to every pot of soup. She grows them in her cellar. Her secret is sea water: two parts of that to every three parts taken from the tap. Seaweed. Sea mist. The secret is the heavy pan she uses, made for her out of boiler iron by a ship's engineer as a token of his devotion. Its metal is not stable, but leaks and seeps its unrequited love into the soup. Her secret is the special fish that's caught for her by an old man, at night. He rows out beyond the shipping lanes, anchors in the corridor of moonlight, and scoops them from the water in a kitchen colander. Or else the magic's in the vegetables. Or in some expensive, esoteric spice.

'Why all the fuss?' she asks, as the visitors depart. 'Is not all soup the same?'

Yet now, at night, when we are going home, we sometimes smell the putrefying truffles from the street, or catch a glimpse of moonlit rowing boats, or look into her kitchen at the back end of the house to see her lifting her lovelorn sailor's pan on to the hob, or hear the tidal rhythms of the sea as two-parts brine goes by its secret route into her soup. We find her carrying something – skeins? – across the room. They could be wool or seaweed skeins. We cannot tell. We see her fingers in the steam, adding magic touches to the stock. We see her sleight of hand, the charms she uses to entice these strangers to her rooms.

So, for a month or two – for fame is brief and fashions only fleeting – our tables at the celebrated restaurant are taken by new visitors to town. And we must wait – yes, wait and see – until its reputation fades, until there's room again for us to sit and smoke, to dine and feel at home, to dip our spoons and bread into this new and famous mystery.

46

We were away ten days. In our absence, something must have shifted in our house, a quake, a tilt, a ghostly hand, a mischievous intruder, some global subsidence. It was enough to make the freezer door swing open. Maybe only slightly at first, just wide enough to fill the kitchen with gelid air. But once the frozen food inside began to defrost, to shed its cold paralysis, the packets and the bags became unstable. They sank and fell against the partly open door. They avalanched. Some packets tumbled out and hit the boards. The wildlife in our house had cause to celebrate. Heaven had provided manna on the kitchen floor and lots of time to feed on it. The distant glacier had calved some frozen meals for all the patient arthropods.

When we returned, the smell was scandalous, a nauseous conspiracy of vegetables and meats and insect waste. The rats had defecated everywhere. The larder slugs had filigreed their trading routes. Someone had left a green-blue mohair sweater inside the freezer, knitted out of mould. The broken flecks of wool were maggot worms and wax-moth larvae. The sweater seemed to shrug and breathe with all the life it held.

We shrugged and cursed. This was the worst of welcomes. We put on rubber gloves, got out the cleaning rags and mops, filled up a bucket with disinfectant and hot water, set about the task of clearing up the food, of pulling out the emerald body from the freezer, of closing once again the slightly open door.

Within an hour we'd restored the ice. Unless you looked inside the empty freezer, saw the lack of frozen food, you'd never guess that we'd been breached and burgled by the teeming universe.

47

We were brought up not to eat the cores. To do so was considered greedy, messy, ill-mannered and, we were assured, immensely dangerous. Vitalized by our digestive juices and the dark, the pips would swell and strike. An apple tree would spring up and flourish in the warm loams of our intestines 'like a baby', until its roots and branches spread and burst out of our sides. Our skins and clothes would tear apart. 'Then you'll be sorry,' mother said.

The only cure, if any pips were to be defiantly swallowed by any of her girls, was a dose of weedkiller and, possibly, if that did not prevent germination, a painful operation with a pair of secateurs. 'It's not a story I've made up,' she said. 'Go down to the orchard and you'll see how true it is. Look for the faces and the hands of the boys and girls who've swallowed cores. They've turned into bark.'

I hated orchards then, and apples too. I did not want to end up like the children I'd discovered in the bark, hard and sinewy, distorted by pain, with ants and beetles crawling on their eyes and nothing to protect them from the night.

These days I have recovered from my mother's house. I always chew the cores. I do not spit the pips into my palm. Indeed, as I grow older, the thought of something new and green, striking life inside me, growing 'like a baby', is not a nightmare any more. I rather think that orchards are a better resting place than cemeteries or crematoria. I'd sooner finish as a piece of bark than ash or bone.

I used to tell my only son, 'Eat the cores. They're the healthiest bit.' He did as he was told. Frightened, I suppose, of being ill. But he's defiant now, I find. Today we drove my grandchildren to school. They had their breakfasts on the hoof. An apple each. I watched them chewing up against the cores like hamsters. I did not dare speak. My son rolled down the windows of the car. 'Go on,' he said. 'See how far they'll go.' A family ritual, I am sure. They waited till we reached the open land, between the fast road and the shops. And then the cores went out, flung fast and wide.

'There'll be an orchard there before you know it,' their father said. 'Those pips are apple trees.'

48

This was the second time she'd died in bed. It was her second burial as well. Nine years before the funeral, the hillside – undermined by summer rain and quarrying – had slipped and piled itself against our neighbour's house as quietly as a drift of snow. She and her husband were fast asleep, exhausted by a day of harvesting, their suppers still uneaten at their sides. The boulder clay had shouldered all its strength against their stone back wall until their room capsized and the contents of the attic and the flute-tiled roof collapsed on to their bed. My neighbour dreamed, fooled for an instant by the sudden weight across her legs, that the dogs had jumped up on the eiderdown. This was against the farmhouse rules. She was ready in her sleep to knock them back on to the bedroom floor.

Now she and her husband were not sleeping. But they were trapped beneath their sheets, beneath the eiderdown, by rubble from the land and from the house and so could only stay exactly where they were, their heads and chests protected by a porch of beams and timbers, their legs encased by cloth and clay. A stroke of luck. They had been saved from instant death by ceiling beams, stout wood from local trees. They had woken in a dark and sudden tent, closed off from the world.

By dawn the heat was stifling. They tore their night-clothes off and ripped the sheets. They called for help but could tell from the way their voices were absorbed that they would not be heard. They knew that their uneaten supper was within reach. Except there was no reach for them. They could not turn or stretch. The earth was just a finger-length away. They breakfasted on perspiration from their lips and moisture from the clay.

By evening the clay had fixed and baked, entirely dry. They sweated only smells. No moisture any more, and nothing on their lips to drink. They should have died within a day; the heat, the pain, the thirst would put an end to them. But they had worked their whole lives with clod and clay and stone and knew their properties. A thousand times, to stave off hunger in the middle of a task, the old man had popped a pebble into his mouth and sucked. He swore that he could always taste what crop was in the field. So now he searched the rubble with his one free hand until he found the flat, impassive flanks of stones, the ones he'd hauled so many times out of the way of his motor plough. He tugged two stones the size of supper plates free of the clay with his strong fingers and placed one on his wife's naked stomach and the other on his own. The weight expelled the danger, saved their lives. Their fevers were absorbed by stones. And once the stones had levelled off at body temperature, they were discarded by my neighbours and colder thermostats were found.

The old man and his wife stayed strong with stones. Their bodies grew as gelid as the earth and they could feel their stomachs filling, the slow transfusion into them of rain and sun and harvest crops.

The diggers finally came with dogs to hunt for bodies. Who could survive that long and in that heat with nothing to sustain them? But when they pulled the rubble and the rocks away and peered between the ceiling beams they saw at once how hale the couple seemed, sustained in their hot tent. Each had a flat stone on the abdomen, as if their bodies would have drifted off, would have risen through the earth and rubble, as sinuous and weightless as a plume of smoke, without the anchoring of stones.

'You can't eat stones,' the farmers always said when crops were poor or prices low. But, when my neighbours had been rescued from the slip, wise heads explained what everybody always knew, that there was sustenance in rock and earth, that those grey stones had fed the couple, by paying for their body heat with food.

And so, those nine years down the line, when the old man had to put his wife into the ground for good, he did not send her off clutching family photographs or her best brooch or something gold to bribe the gods or (as is often done) put cobs of maize into her hands to feed her in the afterlife. Instead, he placed one of the flat grey stones that had once saved her life across her abdomen and wrapped her fingers round its rim. The stone, he thought, might return its heat to her and once again might sweat its nutrients and minerals, its energies, on to her skin, to be absorbed, to keep her warm and hale and fed until the rubble and the clay backed off, replaced the roof, restored the rear wall to their lives, returned uphill from whence it came.

49

'The finest food, like the best of marriages, is bound to break the rules,' according to Eugene Naval. 'It seeks to reconcile opposing tastes and textures, sweet with sour, hot with cold, sharp with bland, the fluid and the firm, the solemn and the comic, and it depends as much on luck as diligence.'

So the tiny Syrian who, when we were kids, used to run the fried-food stall down by the harbour esplanade was working in the best traditions of his craft when – by way of cleaning up and as a joke aimed only at himself – he made a meal of his remaining scraps one afternoon, combining the last fish on his tray and a sorry piece of lamb's liver with the one surviving wheel of pineapple. He frittered the lot in sesame oil, wrapped it in a left-over sour pancake, added a dash of unsold onion relish and a dramatic shake of Boulevard Cream Liqueur from his near-empty bottles, and garnished everything with hissop leaves.

He would have tested it himself, then tossed it to the gulls, had not the seminary tutor come cycling by and, tempted by the new and usual smells, stopped off for an unscheduled snack.

'I'm closing up. There's nothing left,' the Syrian explained, but the tutor could see for himself that this was not entirely true. He bought the pancake full of scraps – a melange which as yet had not been named – described its smell as 'heavenly', donated a copy of the most recent *Seminarian*, of which he was the proud editor, and rode off on his bike.

Depending on your viewpoint, the tutor tumbled off his bike that afternoon, fifty metres from the Syrian, either because the pioneering snack was so fabulously delicious, or because it was too shockingly extravagant for one who earned a living advocating moderation and austerity. It's possible, of course, that he simply lost balance, fell and stunned himself. It couldn't have been easy for a man of his age and weight, and with so many people strolling on the esplanade, to grip the handlebars and eat his pancake at the same time.

What is certain is that the Syrian, delighted at the impact he had made on someone of another faith and size, incorporated this new pancake meal of liver, fish and pineapple into his regular menu. The passengers from visiting liners took word of it back to their chefs at home, and it appeared in restaurants and cookery books from that time on.

So even though the Syrian never became rich or famous, he made a lasting contribution to international cuisine. But only he – and those of us out walking near the harbour on that afternoon in 1969 – can say with any certainty why this distinguished snack is known throughout the world as 'tutor on two wheels' and, incidentally, why the proud seminarian himself was from that day onwards fêted as 'the Pancake'.

50

What could be a better wedding gift for two dear friends? A newly germinated love-leaf tree for the glassed-in balcony of their first apartment. It was, in fact, a sort of palm, *Roystonea labia*. We did not know whether they were green-fingered but, never mind, they'd have to care for it. The label in the pot described our gift as 'edible, low-maintenance and with a modest habit, 2 metres at ten years.' What caught our eye, though, were the claims made by the sales leaflet that came with every purchase. It said:

The inner meat, shoots and tender terminal buds of the lip palm, or love-leaf tree, from Madagascar can be harvested as a vegetable and eaten as a dressed salad or with rice-and-pork dishes. Tradition forbids the picking of the foliage before or after the palm's seventh birthday. Shoots of a seven-year-old plant, also known as heart of palm, *palmetto d'or* or millionaire's salad, are, however, thought to bring good fortune and rejuvenation to their consumers and are regarded as potent aphrodisiacs.

With this growing gift, then, we'd plant a time bomb in their marriage. Here was a loving meal, seven years in preparation, to whet their appetites.

The lip palm flourished on their balcony. We checked whenever we went round, that first year of their marriage. The leaves were glossy and unpicked, the soil was damp, the plant was growing up. We envied them the hungry years ahead. We were aroused ourselves, just at the prospect of the harvest on their seventh anniversary.

It is a miracle they've stayed together for so long. They've both got other friends and lovers. We never see them in each other's company, not even in the shops or at the railings of the school. Their love was so short-lived. There was no heart to it. It has to be the little girl – she's six this year – that stops them splitting up.

We went round to their place about a week ago, to babysit. Their daughter was asleep by nine. We must both have had the same thing on our mind. We'd done our sums. The lip palm was seven. We went out on to their balcony like thieves, armed with a kitchen knife. I think it was a shock, a disappointment, too, to find the centre of their tree removed. They must have cut and eaten the meat, we guessed – too good to waste – and gone off in their separate cars to spend their resurrected passions with more recent friends.

We managed to cut out what remained of the freshest

shoots and foliage. We did not bother with the salad dressing or the pork and rice. We ate palmetto, on the balcony, like chocolate. How good it was! How young we felt as, with their daughter sleeping in a distant room, we did what two dear friends should do when they have passed their seventh, loving year.

51

It's said that cheese is milk that has grown up, fresh milk transformed by time. If so, then what is boysie tart? A senile dish, turned bitter by the years? It's made from old, blue cheese, matured – ignored – enough to be as hard and slippery as a horse's hoof.

The cheese is difficult, too gnarled to cut easily. You can only chisel and pare it into hard slivers, the devil's nail clippings. It won't be edible until you've baked it with sultanas, prunes and well-hung game – a scrub fowl's best – in a sourdough case. Old cheese, old fruit, old yeast, old meat. All carcasses. For New Year's Eve, the last meal of the dying year.

If you've an orange that's gone hard and turned to parchment, then squeeze what reasty juice remains on to the tart. Then dine the old year out, with timid forks, with ancient friends. This is the taste of those dishonoured resolutions that have left their pungent marks throughout the house, those perfidies that have the gift of ageing cheese, and souring yeast, and shrivelling the plums and grapes, and putrefying meat.

Tomorrow is another year. Fresh milk.

52

Ours is a little town of great, historic charity. In the last six months alone, public subscription has put a new roof on the medieval chapel, and planted a garden for the blind, and raised the money to buy a touring bus for the use of local schools. We have made holiday provisions for fifteen pensioners and sent coach parties to the zoo. The park is somewhat overburdened with cedar benches and flowering trees, donated to the town by dutiful relatives in memory of a parent or a child. The street fête in the summer raises money for the lame, the hungry and the orphaned, who limp and starve and grieve in places that we can't pronounce. The cottage art museum, up in the pines, has just acquired a small Matisse, thanks to the efforts of our citizens.

So it ought to come as no surprise that when three refugee families were dumped like sodden cargo on the docks one night they were quickly offered temporary housing in the block behind the port by the Association for the Poor. And somebody (she much prefers to stay unnamed) began to organize a 'cart'. In other words, the open trailer, used by the private school for taking camping expeditions to the hills, was draped with lights and dragged around the better streets by some of the older pupils to gather food for our new visitors.

To start it off, the one-who-wants-to-stay-unnamed went to her own larder and removed a large and almost full jar of mixed pickles. Her husband, a heartburn martyr and the owner of the school, could not – she was weary of reminding him – risk eating pickles any more. She cleaned the inside of the glass rim with a cloth, disguised the pierced jar top with a cap of green muslin held in place by a matching rubber band, and put her offering on to the cart. The boarding master, a divorcee of eighteen months, came out from his flat and rid himself at last of his wife's exotic teas.

The first house that they reached provided half a dozen tins of fruit in heavy syrup. 'Glad to help,' the woman said. She was a kilo overweight and had determined, only that morning, to cut down on sugary desserts. The next house offered a packet of unpopular breakfast cereal, hardly touched. And the next, a cellophane packet of spaghetti shapes, which had hardened and lost much of their colour in the months since they'd been bought. The next, a red string sack of onions, podgy-skinned and coiffed with dying yellow shoots. And then a bottle of the local wine (which no one from the region drinks) and, finally (from the last house in the street), the well-intentioned but not entirely edible fig cake that the daughter had prepared at school a day or two before. 'We ate it all up for lunch,' her mother would explain. 'And it was wonderful.'

The second street quickly yielded its offerings of rusty tins, odd-smelling packets thought too old to use, flat lemonade, three cartons of Fortified Meals for the elderly (no longer needed by a recently buried aunt), dried pulses smooth and solid as porcelain, yoghurt well beyond its date, the unused ingredients of too ambitious meals, unwanted gifts, imported goods with no translation on the label, hasty choices, past mistakes. And so on, downtown from the school, street after street, until the cart was overloaded with our charity and had become the oddest shopping trolley in the world.

Here is the photograph. The pupils are lined up behind the cart. Three little waifs are posing on their month of meals. The owner of the school is shaking hands with a wildly grinning refugee. The caption says the town donated 200 kilos to its 'unfortunate guests'.

And that's not counting all the problems solved, and all the larders tidied up at last, the daughters satisfied, the heartburns eased, the diets honoured, the separations finalized, and the blunders of the past concealed as gifts.

53

What's for dinner? *Pig's cheese*. Always the same reply. And what's for pudding? *Buttered stones and acorns*. And what's to drink? *Chicken milk*. What's for breakfast, if we stay that long and don't run home to mum in tears? *Scrambled goat eggs on toast*.

We never needed calling twice for meals.

But then my grandma always disappointed us with stews and roasts and apple tarts. Undramatic food that we could trust. Things we had at home. The sort of lunches that they dished up at school. Yet still we used to live in hope. We'd look out from her downstairs room, on those always rainy days when we stayed at the farm, and watch the two of them at work between the barns. Soon my grandma would return, wet through, her trugs and punnets full of food.

From that farmhouse window with its peeling paint, its ornaments, its wind-thinned glass, we saw the chickens and the pigs contesting for the kitchen waste. We saw the great oak trees refusing to relinquish even one centimetre to the wind. We watched the line of tethered goats picking at their nests of leaves. How easily their devil's hooves might crack and spill our eggs. Behind the house the tipping field was dappled with the yellow, plough-turned stones. And on the hill-beyond-the-hill, the furthest field, my grandpa's ewes were always lifting in the wind.

And what would make our feast on Christmas Day? Always the same reply. *Sheep wings.*

54

The devil wanders with his straw sack at night through
the meadows and the woods behind the town. He's there,
we're told, to plant the mushrooms that he's raised in hell,
where there's no light to green them, so that the gatherers
who come at dawn, against the wisdoms of the country-
side, can satisfy their appetites for sickeners or conjurers
or fungi smelling of dead flesh and tasting of nothing
when they're cooked. He feeds them disappointments,
nightmares, fevers, indigestion, fear. He lets them breakfast on his spite.

The mushroom devil has been seen from time to time.
Courting couples seeking privacy in some deep undergrowth have heard his foot snap stems behind them or
sensed him creeping by their cars, a mocking voyeur
hoping to disrupt their love. Those midnight wanderers
who search for mysteries and gods when all the bars have
shut have told how he has come so close that he has

stunned them with his breath. He shows himself to children, too. They run out of the woods and fields, their punnets empty, their bikes abandoned, with the devil at their tails.

Those foolish ones who stand and stare report his backing gait, his clumsiness. He has the odours of a kennel, plus boiled eggs, scorched hair and sweat, they say. They cannot capture him. He will not talk or give his name. He slips away, enveloped by the unresisting darkness. But first he holds his open sack for them to see and smell the rootless puffballs and the chanterelles, the honey funguses, the magic heads, the ceps, the shagcaps, boletes, morels, the inky dicks, which he will push into the earth that night like unconvincing garden ornaments.

Sometimes they only see his stooping back and watch his white hands coming from his sack.

I, too, have met the devil in the woods. I, too, have seen the mushrooms in his bag, lolling like eviscerated parts, meringues of human tissue, sweetbreads, smelling of placenta and decay. To tell the truth, these mushrooms baffle me. I've eaten them in many of their forms, I've tried the best, but always I am bored by them. The moment that you take them from the earth, they're dull. The moment that you place them in your mouth, they let you down. I've always thought they were expensive and absurd. If they've been planted by the devil, then he is making fun of us.

So I was curious when he and I crossed paths. I followed him. He let me follow him, for he is not afraid of us. He turned his back on me and didn't care. I watched his antics in the night. I watched his white hands and his sack. And

I can tell you, he has fooled you yet again. The devil is not emptying his sack, but filling it. He does not plant. He picks, he picks, he picks. That's why his back is bent. He is the one who wants the mushrooms for himself. His greed is stronger than his spite. He thinks the mushrooms are too good for us. We'd not appreciate the poisons or the tangs that they provide, their blasphemies. We are too dull and timid for the magic and the flesh. He roams the woods and meadows when it's dark to satisfy himself. He knows which mushrooms to pull up. The ones he leaves for us are flavourless.

55

Here is an average restaurant. Each Sunday, we take our seats to order omelettes and to watch the chef present our mussels to the visitors. He has become the weekend entertainment of the town. There's nothing else to do – except in church, or ten miles up the coast, away from friends and family.

Last summer (so the chef reports) a politician from the state drove through. The woman with him couldn't be his wife. They sat right there, next to the window, with a sideways view down to the port. He ordered local produce for her ('I always dine from the region,' he said. 'That's how you end up with the simplest and the freshest food.' The cheapest, too). They'd have the brandied aubergines to start with – oily, cold, lascivious – and then the pork stew and a bottle of the earthy, hillside wine that no one from the region drinks. You can imagine what he had in mind for her – what with the alcohol, the aphrodisiacs, his hand pushed out across the table top to stroke her painted fingernails, the showing off.

A little ancient jealousy from chef, perhaps, explains what happened next. The politician only wanted to impress his guest and not be made a fool of by the food. He had a point. The wine bottle was insufficiently chilled, he complained. The bread (served in one of the yellow, woven-plastic baskets that gave the restaurant its name) was 'not today's'. The aubergine was bitter. Had no one in the kitchens degorged it with salt before they dished it up? Did they employ a comic or a cook?

The waiter at that time (a student long since gone up north with one of our town's better-looking girls) returned the wine and the dish of aubergine to the kitchens. 'I heard!' chef said. 'So give them my apologies. And they can have two dozen mussels on the house.'

Oh, surely, everybody knows that our mussels can be dangerous, particularly at that time of the year. The tides are far too weak in summer to clear the soup of sewage from the banks. Dead shellfish decompose more thoroughly when it is warm. So was it just bad luck that nearly all the mussels that finished up on that free dish were treacherous?

Now, this is supposition. No one truly knows exactly how the lovers spent their afternoon. It's possible, of course, that their intestines had been lined with steel and that the sifted toxins of our lavatories passed through without effect. But where's the anecdote in that? We'd rather have the chef's report in which (and God knows how chef knew) the politician and his lunch guest had hardly reached the hotel down the coast when justice called. It might have seemed to other guests or to the ever-patient clerk that their eagerness to reach the room was simple summer lust. But no, they were too pinched about the haunches and too self-involved to be true lovers. And no, his hands were shaking at the lock with something more disruptive – and less fleeting – than desire. Inside at last, alone, they would have tussled for the sink and toilet seat, her skirt half up, his trousers down, but not for the reasons they had planned.

Indeed, the politician had been right to ask; the chef was more a comic than a cook. The stories that he served were better than the food. He made good soufflé out of lies. He made bad soufflé out of eggs. And so, while we might only risk the omelettes or grilled fish on our visits to the Yellow Basket, we never tired of his stories of revenge, or hearing him reproduce on the expresso machine the sound those depth-charged stomachs must have made when his rogue mussels were propelled into the hotel room that summer afternoon. We didn't mind the repetitions, or that he would always illustrate the colour of the diners' skin by holding a lime up to the light, or that some of the details changed – improved – with each retelling.

Was it, then, simply to please himself or to keep us in his thrall (and in his restaurant) that chef announced at the beginning of this season that mussels would be served 'by way of an apology' more regularly at the Yellow Basket? He says that he can tell which mussels will be troublesome. The safe ones snap shut at once if they've been prised open with a fork. The dead ones don't. Others to avoid are those with shells that have unhinged before being cooked, and any that do not fall open to accept the sacrament of garlic butter and parsley once (according to his recipe) they have been roasted in hot ash. All these unworthy ones are set aside for chef's selected guests. Perhaps he's only teasing us, but still we have to – want to – swallow all his words.

They look so innocent, those blue-black castanets, their pearly inner cases and their fat, grey beans of meat. But they have caused, this year, a banker from America to spoil his trousers and the front seat of his car. And they have packed their dark export of bacteria into the luggage of at least three lady pensioners from the cruise liner, which puts into our port on its round trip each spring. The on-board doctor almost had to have one of the women lifted off by helicopter. And the chef's apology has given the sweats, the vomits and the chills, the cramps and the diarrhoea to one lone diner from Milan, two German boys, a family of five with noisy children, a Princeton graduate, a priest, the owner of a smart boutique in France, a couple planning a divorce, several state executives and (according to the chef) a gastronomic writer from *The New York Times* magazine. It was as if we'd made these strangers pregnant. They'd gone away with our dull, revengeful town inside. And they'd rebirthed our mussels down the coast.

So, as we lift his omelette to our mouths each Sunday lunchtime, we pray for troublemakers. We pray that chef will be offended by his passing visitors, that they'll complain, that he will offer his apologies and speak those paralysing words, 'I hope you will accept a plate of mussels on the house.' We do not like to stare, of course, but it is hard to resist a sideways look from time to time. We want to see the empty shells pile up.

So this is how an average restaurant can always have its tables occupied.

But best of all is on the street, when the driver of too large a car, or the possessor of an accent we don't like, or merely someone who appears too fortunate inquires, 'Where is a decent place to eat?' It is a duty and a joy to point and say, 'The Yellow Basket. Up above the port. The mussels are quite good, I hear. *Bon appétit.*' An unexpected opportunity.

We're cruel, of course. We're unforgivable. Why should we punish them simply for coming from a different place or having better lives or being on vacation? The pleasure that we get when we imagine how they'll pass their afternoons is hardly warranted. We know our laughter is malicious – but surely there's some justice in it too.

We feel as if we've cast a heavy stone on to the all-too-perfect surface of the sea, to send our ripples out against the waves.

56

Everybody – rich or poor – had soup stones in those days. I found ours a half an hour's bike ride out of town on what, before the container port was built, used to be Crescent Beach. I had to wet my shoes and trouser legs to retrieve it from the plunging tide. Amongst the million grey-white granite rocks, it caught my eye, distinguished by a circling band of black, which made the stone appear as if it had been split in two then fixed with tar gum. It was a glinting and dramatic gem, still wet in that hard light, a perfect fit in my small hand.

It was less glinting when I got home that afternoon. The granite had dried and dulled. A half an hour from the sea was all it took to rob my stone of light. But still I prepared it for my mother's kitchen, full of hope. You had first to boil the ocean out, or else your soups would always taste of fish.

My mother used that stone in every soup she made. She

couldn't make good soup without its help, she said. The flavours wouldn't mix. The bottom of the pot would burn or stick. The ingredients would tumble on the heat and boil over. A soup without a stone was as heartless as a peach or plum without a stone. But with its help, she claimed, she could even make good soup out of just tap water. No stock, no meats, no vegetables. Perhaps the granite had a flavour of its own. We'd have to try one day. Perhaps it stored a memory and aftertaste of everything that had ever shared its pot.

Whenever she made soup and I was home, she used to let me add my piece of granite to the pot before she lit the gas. And, when the soup was cooked, it was my job to take the colander spoon and lift the soup stone out. I used to marvel at its fleeting smell and how it had briefly regained the light and colour of the beach.

I keep the family soup stone on the windowsill of my apartment now. I haven't cooked with it for years. Who makes soups these days? There's such a choice of ready-mades in shops. Occasionally I use the stone as a pocket companion for travelling, a granite talisman to keep the plane from crashing, but otherwise I hardly notice it. Except sometimes, when I'm reminded of home, I run my soup stone underneath the tap to bring the smells and colours out, the beach, the sea-tricked light, the gems of silica, the small boy stepping in the tumbling tide, retrieving flavours for his mother's thousand soups.

57

His breath was damp and earthy. The old man had tuber-
ous growths in his gut. Doctor Gregor could palpate them
with his palm. They were starchy, as tough as carrots.
'There is some inflammation,' he said. 'Nothing to worry
about. Rest is what you need.' What was the point of
alarming a man of eighty-two with an honest diagnosis,
with hospitals, with surgery? He would be dead within the
month. 'Are you in any pain?' The old man shook his head.
The doctor prescribed warm olive oil to 'ease the passage
through your bowel'.

He did not die within the month. He lasted ten more
months before he came to Doctor Gregor's clinic again. It
was the spring of the drought. He looked as tough and
sinewy as a man of half his age. Indeed, he looked a little
younger than before, though he was eighty-three now.

'Are you in any pain?' the doctor asked again.

'A little. Once in a while.' When he bent to tie his boots,

he explained, or tug at weeds, the hard knots in his stomach bunched against the waistband of his trousers. It was uncomfortable. What man of eighty-three could bend to touch his boots without a little pain?

'I think I'd better take a look,' the doctor said. He helped the old man on to the examination bed and turned him on to his side, his face towards the wall. He pulled on a pair of disposable lubricated gloves. 'Knees up. This shouldn't take a second. Think of somewhere nice.'

The old man searched for somewhere nice. At first it was the modest garden where he now lived in town: the tiny square of lawn, the hem of evergreens, the single potted maple on the patio. But soon he settled on the larger piece of land that he had owned when he was younger, its trees, its stony paths, its dogged thistles, its flinty earth, the vegetables, which he would harvest on summer Sundays and bring up to the house in a trug.

The doctor did not have to penetrate too deeply beyond the sphincter to find the woody growths in his patient's bowel. Perhaps they were elephantine polyps of some kind, and not a string of cancers. Perhaps they were benign. Clearly they caused no pain, except when the old man stooped to touch his toes. Doctor Gregor pushed against the lowest tumour with his index finger. It did not seem attached, but moved freely. Its shape was odd. It was not symmetrical or funnelled, but complex, with extensions and recessions like the chambered plaster cast of an earth-roach burrow. 'Have you examined your stool of late? Anything unusual? Any blood?' The old man shook his head. Why would he want to examine his stool?

The doctor was not a sentimental or a squeamish man.

He managed to work a couple of small 'polyps' loose. He put one in a lidded specimen tub and labelled it with a date and a reference for the laboratories. The other he put in a sterile bag with a little purified water. He was puzzled, but doctors are often puzzled. Let the laboratories give a name to it. He put his arm around the old man's shoulders and took him to the door. 'Warm olive oil,' he said.

Laboratories can take a month to analyse and process specimens. Doctor Gregor did not think the matter urgent enough to telephone for their report. The old man was fit for eighty-three. What was a month to him? They'd get their answers soon enough. In fact the old man died within three weeks of his last visit to the surgery. A sudden and unheralded stroke, too quick to experience. A neighbour called the doctor out one morning and led him to the body. His patient must have died the evening before. He'd been standing in his tiny garden with a hose. The grass and shrubs were green with care, despite the weeks of drought. The tap had been running all night long. The old man lay on his back in shallow water. Slugs were on his shirt and trousers, taking refuge from the flood. There was a smell – damp and earthy like the old man's breath had been. It was the smell of vegetation. So that was that. He'd made a decent age and met a decent death.

The laboratories sent their report and their invoice. The old man's specimen was described as 'non-invasive', 'benign', and 'entirely vegetable: water 83%; albuminoids 2%; gum 9.1%; sugar 4.2%; inulin 1.1%'. Doctor Gregor held the 'polyp' he had kept up to the light in its sterile bag. It seemed more swollen. The inside of the bag was silvery with condensation. He paid the laboratory bill by cheque. A waste of time and money. He could not pass the costs on to a patient now. He put the swelling polyp on his windowsill. He did not like to part with it, now that the man was dead.

Encouraged by the heat and light and by the purified water, the vegetable grew a pair of tiny yellow horns. Its wrinkles flattened. Its extensions and recessions achieved a kind of nippling puberty. One horn pinkened, lengthened and uncurled. The old man's polyp had a shoot. The doctor put it in a glass dish on a bed of damp toilet paper. He watered it each day. He gave it houseplant feed. Quite soon he had three green shoots and two more horns. Roots as thin as cotton thread clung to the damp paper. He had to pick a greenfly from its stem.

A patient – asked to lean against the windowsill while Doctor Gregor checked her damaged vertebrae – recognized it as a tuber. Not a tumour, then?

'I've never grown these ones myself,' she said. 'It's root ginger, isn't it? Or Jerusalem artichoke? What do they taste like? Does it smell?'

The doctor held it to his nose. The old man's breath again.

'You'll have to pot it up,' the patient said. 'It won't survive on that!'

The doctor sent his nurse out to the shops to buy a pot and some compost. He thumbed the polyp into the soil, and only damaged a couple of shoots. He put the plant outside the front door of his surgery. His patients dropped their cigarette ends into the pot, or spat into the soil. The soil flourished on bronchitis. It put up three good stems, with heavy leaves, and – in the summer – three inconspicuous yellow flowers at shoulder height. The old dears coming in for their pills didn't have to bend to press their noses to the blooms. The yellow petals were busy with weevils. His patient's diagnosis was confirmed by some of the many gardeners on the doctor's list: they were Jerusalem artichokes – or Canadian potatoes as one man called them – not root ginger.

In September, the three stems and their leaves dried out and died. They broke away, and the pot became an ashtray, nothing else. In November, Doctor Gregor found a moment to carry the pot through to the yard behind the surgery. He turned the soil out on to a plastic bag. He planned to wash the pot and plant a basil in it, or a daphne. Something colourful or evergreen for the steps. There were a dozen clusters of the old man's polyps multiplying in the soil, a starchy kilo at the very least. The doctor picked them out and put them in the emptied pot. They smelled of soot. 'More trouble than they're worth,' his nurse remarked. 'Except in soup!'

That night, he took the crop to his apartment. He did not peel them or attempt to scrape them. They were too oddly shaped. He scrubbed half of them in warm water. He cooked them au gratin with bacon curls. His brother and his sister-in-law came for dinner. The Jerusalem artichokes, he said, were the gift of a patient: 'He grew them himself.' They tasted bland and floury. According to his sister-in-law, they would have benefited from a pinch of coriander, say, or more salt.

Doctor Gregor was fond of his brother and his wife, but she was far too keen to give advice on what would benefit his life, his work, his apartment, his cooking. More salt. A dab of paint. A housekeeper. A bit of colour to his clothes. A holiday. A wife. 'Why don't you settle down?' Or, 'Find a woman for yourself. That nurse of yours is quite a decent sort.'

The doctor showed his brother and his wife to the door. He let them take the half-kilo of Jerusalem artichokes that had not been scrubbed and cooked. For their kitchen garden.

His guests were a little windy from their meal. Their breaths were damp and earthy. 'They're nice, but indigestible,' his brother said.

'Are you in any pain?' Doctor Gregor asked. 'Take warm olive oil, to ease their passage through your bowels.' He wondered if he should have said more about the artichokes, how natural, how death-defying and how benign they were.

The doctor's brother dug the tubers into a trench of flinty earth, amongst the dogged thistles at the bottom of their garden. He put in lime and compost. In summer there were yellow flowers, and in autumn there were tubers by the kilo. On Sundays he would harvest them and bring his trug of starchy vegetables up into the house. They made the perfect Monday soup, which kept them warm and bilious in winter.

58

You'll need a liturgy and a medium pan, a hen's egg, some bread, some salt, a knife, a spoon, the kitchen to yourself. Put the egg in water over a medium flame. Find, at once, the 37th hymn, God's way of timing eggs, and when the water starts to boil begin to sing. Not too briskly. *Moderato* all the way. Sing all three verses and the chorus lines. The hymn is timed to suit the egg.

Make as much noise as you want. Belt out the words: 'And on this rock Our church will stand,/A gateway to the Promised Land.' The final word's 'amen', of course, two sinking syllables beyond the tune. The amen is the point when yolk and shell and albumen become discrete.

Now spoon the amen egg out of the pan, decapitate it with a knife. You'll find the flesh is cooked exactly to your taste, the white precisely firm, the yolk still bright and viscous, the smell of hell and sulphur on the air – as you would wish whenever you sing hymns.

59

Easter Day. The village custom was for everyone – even those who would not go to church – to spread a handful of flour on a stone as an offering. You could expect the flour to be gone within the hour. Rats and birds would have it. Or else the wind or rain.

We have a misplaced stone next to the gate into the orchard. It's a vagrant, not a local stone – the local stone is silver-grey – but whoever brought it there did so more than eighty years ago. My grandmother remembers it from when she was young. She used to sit her dolls on the flat top and let them watch her stretch out in the grass and read. They were her guardians. The colour of the stone, she says, was like material – velvet, mauve. She had a matching dress and she made matching dresses for her dolls.

That flat top was, of course, the perfect place to put our offering, a gram or so of bleached self-raising flour on a tonne or so of blood-red stone.

It was only because the weather was good and my spirits unusually low that I spent so much time, that Easter, out of doors. Otherwise I might not have witnessed what occurred beneath the canopy of fruit trees. I have to tell you what I saw with my own eyes, something defying science and good sense, in order to convince myself, not you, that sometimes simple things – like flour, sunlight, stone – can break the rules.

I knew that there were rats around. There always are in orchards. I could hear the fretful, constant scurrying of rodent feet. And there were nesting birds for whom the flour ought to provide easy foraging. But, possibly, because I was settled in the grass a metre from the stone, engrossed by the music on my Walkman and by a soothing glass or two of beer, the wildlife kept away on that first day. And when I got up in the afternoon to go back to my parents' house, greatly rested and tranquillized by my half-sleep, I noticed the flour was untouched. Indeed, it seemed to me the volume of the flour had increased, as if it had drawn from the air or from the sun a fortifying trace of heat and moisture.

I do now know what made me turn my empty glass upside down and place it over the flour. I can't imagine that I wanted to protect it from the dew or deny the birds and rats their easy meal. I cannot claim I had an inkling of what might happen overnight. I was just curious to see how long our offering would last if I protected it.

Again, I was not sure when I returned next day if the actual *amount* of flour had increased as it appeared to have done. The *volume* had, of course. The offering had swollen by a centimetre. Anyone could see it had. The risen fl pressed against the sides of the glass. And when I lifted up the glass, its contents were as rubbery as dough, and round. You might say it most resembled a communion wafer.

That second day, encouraged by the unseasonal heat, we both – the offering and I – baked in the sun. Each time I looked, the dough suggested that it had proved itself a little more. Certainly, by lunchtime, the wafer had thickened and enlarged. By late afternoon, when the shadow of our roof and chimney pots was stretched across the chilling grass, the wafer had become a ball of dough. The flour must have located airborne yeast, I thought. What other explanation could there be?

I brought my mother's glass salad cover from the pantry and put it on our mauve stone to cover the ball of dough and save it once again from animals. I dropped a pinch of table salt on to the mix. A blessing of sorts. A petition for good luck. A prayer to end the cruel disruptions of my family life. My parents walked down to the orchard, arm in arm, and laughed at me, my pinch of salt, my simple faith in signs. I'd had too many beers, they said. I was too stressed, too fanciful, I was upset. They'd seen mushrooms, bigger than my dough, spring up in half an hour. Nothing to get excited about. 'Nature's odder than you think. Things grow.'

That night, of course, I had the oddest dreams. Who wouldn't dream at times like these, my marriage on the rocks and me, a refugee from home, reduced to staying in the same bedroom where I had slept when I was small? Who wouldn't dream?

The earth was baking in my dream. It proved to be the hottest day of all, sub-tropical. You had to wear a hat. I was walking down to the orchard gate, fearful, doubting, full of hope. The stone, flattered by the warmth, trembled like a heated coal. It glistened like volcanic jewels. The smell was not volcano though, not sulphur and not ash. The smell was bread, fresh baked. I lifted up the glass protector from the flat top of the stone and touched the crust, the split, chestnut turban of a finished loaf, fresh bread baked out of nothing on the hotplate of the stone, our risen offering, my answered prayer. Beyond the odour of the bread there was a hint of aloe and of myrrh. In my dream I covered up the bread with linen. And then I ran down to the village for the priest to come and witness what I took to be a miracle. That risen loaf's a sign, he said, that everything is well. Our blighted pasts are taken from the cross and rubbed with spices and with oils. Our futures are uncrucified. Things grow.

On the third day, I woke exhausted by my night of dreams and went a little sheepishly down to the long grass by the orchard gate to read and think about the battles and the custodies ahead. My mother's glass salad cover had somehow fallen to the ground and smashed. A disappointment and a shock. The stone itself had shifted too, I thought. A touch displaced.

The day was chilly, damp, not tropical at all. Any trace of resurrected dough had disappeared, of course. My dreams had been misleading, mischievous. There was no evidence. The rats and birds had come and knocked the salad cover to the ground. The rats and birds had dined.

My little daughter, five years old, has come today to rescue me. She puts her dolls up on the flat, mauve stone and they guard over us while we stretch out a metre from the orchard gate and stare into the pages of our open books. And if I turn and sniff the air, as country dwellers always do when weather's on the move, I fancy I can smell a bakery – though, let's be honest, an orchard always smells of bakeries. There's yeast in rotting fruit. There's dough in mulching leaves. Tree bark and fungi stink of bread.

60

Our strangest restaurant, the Air & Light, survived five months before its joke wore thin.

We're not immune in this small town to global trends. So when the food and healthcare magazines were full of stories from Japan about a prana sect that did not eat or drink but lived instead on 'atmosphere', two of our lesser artists, tired of paint and canvasses, installed the front part of an empty shop with tables, chairs and blinding lights. It was, they said, the world's first prana restaurant. Their friends dressed up as customers and waiters. There was a pompous maître d' and pretty tablecloths. Orders were taken. Empty glasses, dishes and plates were delivered to the tables. Passers-by could look through the shop's front window to watch nobody eating anything. It was live art. It was, as well, the liveliest and smartest place in town.

It wasn't long, of course, before outsiders – students mostly – came into the restaurant and filled the empty places, keen to play their part and not be fed. There was a queue of volunteers. What isn't clear is how the perpetrators, instead of closing down after a day or two as they had intended, began to charge for admittance to the Air & Light, a modest table fee at first. But then something much more complex, listed on a bill, including details of the 'atmosphere' provided, quantities of prana consumed, and a local tax of 12 per cent.

The charges made the Air & Light too expensive for the students, but still the tables were packed out each night by the better off, keen to be part of the installation and at the cutting edge of food and art. They tipped quite heavily. But, in a way, they were not cheated. The ambience was wonderful. The restauranteurs let buskers in to entertain the clientele. The waiters were attentive and amusing. The conversation was the most animated in town, and uninterrupted by eating and drinking. The 'meals' were meditative and purifying. And outside, on the street, there was always a deep and noisy audience, hustling for places near the window. If you needed to be noticed, then the Air & Light was the place to go.

Al Pacino, in town to film *The Girder Man*, was photographed being witty with an empty plate. The singer, Tambar, went there and sang an aria, leaning on the till. It was, according to the local radio, the coolest spot to take your girl. By the end of the first month – such is the vulgar power of modernism – determined customers had to book their tables a week in advance.

It was, of course, a splendid comedy – but there were some who claimed that the restaurant, by formalizing diet and restraint, was servicing a greater cause than simply a desire to be amused. The Air & Light combated publicly, they claimed, the countless tyrannies of food. It opened up new channels from the body to the mind. It celebrated emptiness in an otherwise oversated world.

It was a bad mistake, in retrospect, to start the takeaway. It brought the poorer students back and let the street crowd in. There was a lot of jostling between the tables. The waiters could not move around as easily. Conversations were interrupted by the general din. The restaurant soon lost its atmosphere. Such things are delicate. Besides, the lesser artists had grown rich and famous, and bored with labouring till the early hours of the morning without a drop to drink. They wanted to get back to their own work. They'd have no trouble selling their under-coloured paintings now. So they closed the Air & Light without a fuss, and all the smarter, richer people from the town were forced to take their hunger and their patronage elsewhere.

61

Our salted cod has dried and shrivelled through the winter to half its netted weight and a quarter of its thickness. We well remember how we caught it on a line, the three of us, my brothers and I. It needed three to play it in to the boat, though three was hardly enough (for we were tired by then) to lift it in the keep net on to the deck. That fish was strong. We even wished our eldest brother hadn't gone away to God knows where to drink himself insane and difficult. A fourth set of hands – even his – might have made the cod a little more obliging. It felt as if we'd brought a squall on board. We'd caught a storm. Even once we'd split the catch open with our knives and hauled its innards out, our boat still rocked and heaved, though there was hardly any swell that night. Its end was intimate and slow. This fish, we knew without expressing it, was one we'd have to keep for ourselves, not sell.

Now the day has come to cut our cod down from the

rafters of the drying room where, safe from draughts and cats, it has been companion to our overalls and waterproofs since summer. We hope that it will feed us for a week or two. The prospect isn't pleasing, though. A fisherman would sooner not eat fish. It brings bad luck. But we have no choice except to take it down for food. Our boat was washed up in the gale last week and holed. There'll be no more fishing for us, and no income, until the fixing plate we've ordered from the engineers is delivered by truck. And that won't be before the spring has opened up the roads. The snow is deep and treacherous this year.

It is my job to haul the biggest pot out of the workshed and roll it through the snow to the drying room. I have to scrape out shards of time-toughened pitch. It's the pot we use each spring for caulking the seams of our hull and sealing decks. A salted cod this size needs soaking in deep water for a day or two before it's ready for the kitchen. You'd need a chainsaw to cut it now. So I lift the fish free from its hook and cradle it in both my arms, as stiff and lifeless as a leather bag. One brother is enough. It hardly weighs. I put it, head down, in the empty pot next to the hot stovepipes, throw in some handfuls of coarse salt and then turn on the hose until all of the cod, except for its protruding tail, is under water. I stir it in. I lick my hands to check the balance of the water. It tastes as salty as the sea. The cod will have the chance to quiver, swell, resalinate, before we trouble it again.

We should have been more vigilant and checked the progress of the fish each night. The timing of such things is critical. The water and the salt restored the cod more rapidly than we'd expected. That's our excuse. 'Excuses never fed a man,' my father used to say. Our two-week meal doubled its weight and quadrupled its thickness behind our backs. We had only a moment's warning. The three of us were on the slipway, pulling up the kelp for fuel, when we heard the splintering and looked up to see the birch door on the drying room fly back and wedge itself in the snow. Our efforts had revivified the cod, as they'd been meant to. But it did not intend to help us through the hungry weeks ahead. It had the strength to clear the pot, as agile as a salmon, and flap into the open air.

We might have caught it had we been a little closer. But by the time we'd reached the foot of the slope up to our house, the fish, mouth gaping, was halfway to the sea. Good luck was on its side. The tide was in, the hill was steep and slippery. Without the snow the cod might well have torn itself to pieces on the bushes and rocks. The snow, though, was a perfect slide, a wet and speeding cousin to the waves.

We tried to cut our salt cod off by running down on to the beach and wading in. If only we could catch its tail. If only we could lift it in our arms before it reached sea deep enough to float. But once a fish smells the ocean it gathers strength, it quickens. It doesn't need the water even. It can swim in air.

Three brothers, then. A fourth one missing, no address. We're standing on the shoreline in our boots, our boat well holed, the roads impassable, our prospects famishing. We hope to see a final sign of our salt cod, far off. A tail perhaps. A fin. We only spot outlying plumes of surf, a half-encountered squall too distant to be frightening, and then the furrows of an ever-grateful sea.

It is, we say, the perfect meal.

62

She'd heard an actor talking on the radio. He loved his cat. So, when it died, he had the animal cremated and put its ashes in an airtight pot on the condiment and spices shelf. He'd add a tiny pinch of ash each time he made a soup or stew, or a cup of instant coffee. The ashes lasted him three months. They didn't seem to spoil the taste of anything. But it was comforting to have the cat inside, recycled as it were, and purring for eternity. He recommended it for anyone with pets.

When her husband died, she took the actor's route. Cremated him and potted him and put a pinch of him into her meals, like grainy, unbleached salt. She judged that the flavour of these meals suffered slightly from his ashes, to tell the truth. Or maybe that was just a widow's queasiness. But certainly the comfort that she felt was less than she had counted on. She did not feel possessed by him. She did not feel at peace as she had hoped. She was not reconciled with her new solitude. Instead, a small voice piped inside her stomach as she lay in bed at night. It bothered her. Her husband's singing voice, high-pitched and watery. The lyrics were not clear, but then they never had been clear when he was living. No matter what she did he would not stop. His singing would not let her sleep.

The doctor listened with his stethoscope. He hummed the tune and tried to put a name to it. He took his patient's temperature. 'This sort of thing is common,' he said. 'I've heard all kinds of songs from widows of your generation. There's not a medicine to fix it. But I'll say to you exactly what I've told the other women, you can't eat grief. It's far too strong and indigestible. You have to let the grief eat you. You have to let the sorrow swallow you. Then put his ashes in the earth and let him go. Come back and see me in a month or two. By then I bet your husband's voice will only be a memory and you'll be happy with the quieter life that you have earned by loving him.'

63

My daughter asked me, 'Do you think that pasta tastes the same in other people's mouths?' Let's try, I said. You first.

I picked a pasta shell from the bowl, dropped it, red with sauce, on to my tongue and closed my mouth. My lips were pursed as if I was waiting to be kissed. I sat down on the kitchen chair and spread my knees. Come on, I said, trying not to laugh or swallow. Be sensible.

She'd started giggling but struggled to compose herself. She pushed against my stretched skirts and reached my face with hers. It was a kiss of sorts. She had to turn her head like lovers do, invade my lips and hunt the pasta with her tongue. She pushed the shell about inside my mouth and then stepped back, a little shocked by what she'd done, at what I'd let her do.

What do you think? 'Tomato, onion, pesto,' she said, remembering the sauce we'd made. 'And lipstick, too. A sort of cherry flavour. Except for that, it tastes exactly the same as it does in my mouth. Your go.'

   She picked a piece of pasta for herself and put it on her tongue. Again she came between my legs. Again we kissed. My tongue got snagged on her loose tooth. Our lips and noses rubbed, we breathed into each other's lungs, our hair was tangled at our chins. I tasted sauce and toothpaste, I tasted sleep and giggling, I tasted disbelief and love that knows no fear. My daughter tasted just the same as me. We held each other by the elbows while I hunted for the pasta in her mouth.

64

oh honey

By the same author

SIGNALS OF DISTRESS

In the winter of 1836 the *Belle of Wilmington* is wrecked off Wherrytown. The Captain and his American sailors flirt, drink, brawl, repair the damage to their ship ... and inflict fresh damage on the town. Another visitor marooned far from home is Aymer Smith, a man brimming with good intentions both for the *Belle's* black slave cook Otto, and for himself, a virgin and a blunderer in search of a wife.

Amid this haunting, monumental landscape, the hopes and hazards of the Old World are pitched – unforgettably – against the New.

'Fluid, clever and funny, bracing as the English seaside on a gusty winter's day' *Independent on Sunday*

By the same author

ARCADIA

Self-made millionaire Victor wants to leave his mark before he dies. He has no family, no lover, so on his eightieth birthday he decides to create a lasting monument in the city that made his fortune. He will destroy the old marketplace and rebuild it in the shape of Arcadia: a modern utopia of glass and greenery.

'The tallest buildings throw the longest shadows – thus great men make their mark,' Victor's architect tells him. Yet Arcadia's shadow falls more darkly than those around him could imagine ...

'Sentence for sentence, it must be one of the most beautifully written books in years' David Robson, *Sunday Telegraph*

By the same author

QUARANTINE

Two thousand years ago four travellers enter the Judean desert to fast and pray. In the blistering heat and barren rocks they encounter the evil merchant Musa – madman, sadist, rapist, even a Satan – who holds them in his tyrannical power. Yet there is also another, a faint figure in the distance, fasting for forty days, a Galilean who they say has the power to work miracles. Here, trapped in the wilderness, their terrifying battle for survival begins ...

'A marvellous book' *Guardian*

'Dazzling, gritty brilliance ... this is a novel of scorching distinction' *Sunday Times*

'A storyteller of unique gifts' *The Times*

By the same author

BEING DEAD

Baritone Bay, mid-afternoon. Celice and Joseph, married, middle-aged, are lying naked on the coast. They had met and first had sex there as students almost thirty years before. Now they hope to rediscover and rekindle passion in the dunes. But this will be a day for death as well as kisses, a day when murder and eternity will fail to put an end to love . . .

'A triumph . . . one of the most distinctive and talented writers of our time . . . This is a work of near-genius' *Literary Review*

'Magnificent' *Sunday Telegraph*

'Shocking because it is filled with truth. It feels like a classic already' *Time Out*

refresh yourself at penguin.co.uk

Visit penguin.co.uk for exclusive information and interviews with
bestselling authors, fantastic give-aways and the
inside track on all our books, from the Penguin Classics
to the latest bestsellers.

BE FIRST

first chapters, first editions, first novels

EXCLUSIVES

author chats, video interviews, biographies, special
features

EVERYONE'S A WINNER

give-aways, competitions, quizzes, ecards

READERS GROUPS

exciting features to support existing groups and
create new ones

NEWS

author events, bestsellers, awards, what's new

EBOOKS

books that click – download an ePenguin today

BROWSE AND BUY

thousands of books to investigate – search, try
and buy the perfect gift online – or treat yourself!

ABOUT US

job vacancies, advice for writers and company
history

Get Closer To Penguin . . . www.penguin.co.uk